The Power of Mesmerism

and

Laura Middleton

THE POWER
OF
MESMERISM

and

LAURA
MIDDLETON

Anonymous

TWO NOVELS FROM
THE
VICTORIAN UNDERGROUND

Grove Press, Inc., New York

THE POWER
OF MESMERISM

A HIGHLY EROTIC
NARRATIVE OF
VOLUPTUOUS
FACTS AND FANCIES

PRINTED FOR THE NIHILISTS
MOSCOW, 1891

Brackley Hall was a fine old place in the lovely
country of Devon and had been in the possession
of the Etheridges for centuries.

The park was beautifully wooded, and stretched
down on one side to the coast, commanding in all
directions the most enchanting views.

Mr. Etheridge was a man of some forty years of
age, of singularly handsome appearance, and bore
evident traces of the Italian blood which flowed in
his veins. He had the appearance of a man having
strong amorous passions, but his manners were as

gentle as those of a woman, and he was universally popular throughout the whole county.

His wife was a woman of unusual beauty. Descended from an old Spanish family, she had married when but sixteen years of age; Mr. Etheridge having met her at the house of some friends, and as they mutually fell in love with each other, their united entreaties overcame the objection raised on account of her youth, and in fact the warm blood that flowed in her veins had ripened her beauty to an extent almost unusual in those of more phlegmatic races.

She was now in her thirty-fifth year, and in the full zenith of her charms. An exquisitely shaped head graced a neck and shoulders white as alabaster, large liquid eyes, and long drooping lashes, a nose of perfect form, and two ruby pouting lips that seemed made to be kissed.

Her form was magnificent, of commanding height, widely spreading hips, and a bosom of massive proportions, the firmness of which rendered stays entirely unnecessary; a fact that was evident on watching the rise and fall of those two lovely globes, their form being perfectly defined even to the nipples, beneath her well-fitting dress.

Her glance was electric, and it was impossible to meet her look unmoved, she exhaled an atmosphere of voluptuousness of the most maddening force.

Her daughter Ethel, who had left school in Paris but a few months, was the very counterpart of her lovely mother in her leading features. She had just completed her seventeenth year, and was of tall, graceful stature, with a perfect figure. The smallness of her waist contrasted perfectly with the ravishing fullness of bosom and wideness of hips. She had the liquid eyes of her mother, but they were suffused with a humidity that was perfectly maddening, and the expression of every feature of her lovely face and palpitating form spoke of a warmth of temperament and lascivious abandon that would have tempted an anchorite.

On a bright summer afternoon, in the year 18—, father, mother, and daughter were waiting at the railway station, anxiously expecting the arrival of the remaining member of the family, Frank, who, a year older than Ethel, had been finishing his education in Germany, and was now returning to take up his residence at Brackley.

At last the train arrived, and they hardly recognised the handsome, tall, and fine-looking young fellow who leaped out to greet them.

A few hours after reaching the house the parents noted a peculiar change that had taken place in their son. A dreamy languor seemed to have taken possession of him, in place of the exuberant flow of animal spirits that characterised him as a boy. He had a strange habit of looking as though he were endeavouring to read the very thoughts of those with whom he came in contact.

Mrs. Etheridge noticed this particularly, but thinking he was fatigued by his long journey, made no remark. But the most remarkable effect was produced on Ethel; her brother seemed utterly unable to remove his eyes from her. Her singular beauty, and the nameless charm that pervaded her, seemed to have an irresistible attraction for him.

Every time that his eye rested on her she trembled violently, and seemed labouring under some mysterious and powerful influence. Her lovely breasts heaved, and the humidity of her eyes increased, and she still seemed unusually excited after her brother had left the room in order to dress for dinner.

Some friends had been invited to dine, and Frank found himself placed between his mother and sister. He glanced alternately at the two lovely bosoms, well exposed by the low dresses each of them wore; and his face flushed, and he seemed for the moment about to faint, but almost immediately recovering himself, he proceeded with his dinner and joined in the conversation.

In the course of the meal he ventured again to glance at his sister, and as she was leaning forward he saw the lovely valley between those hills of snow.

He accidently pressed his knee against hers, she immediately looked at him fondly, and her breasts rose and fell tumultuously as she mechanically pressed closer to him.

Nothing further happened on this occasion, but they had a most charming evening in the drawing room, and Ethel and Frank seemed to have formed a more than usually close friendship. They had not seen each other for four years, and their reunion seemed a source of the greatest delight to both of them. Mrs. Etheridge also inspired her son with the most intense affection.

Before retiring for the night Frank proposed an early walk on the grounds, as he was anxious to renew his acquaintance with all the spots so attractive to him when a boy, and Ethel joyously assented. Six o'clock was agreed to, which would leave them two good hours until breakfast time.

When Ethel retired to rest she was in a state of wild excitement and could not banish her darling brother's image from her thoughts.

At length she fell into a troubled sleep, and after tossing wildly about, awoke suddenly and found that she was spending, her nightdress and chemise were saturated, and her lovely cunt was throbbing with the extasy. She was no stranger to this sensation (as the reader will subsequently learn), as she habitually produced the result with her fingers; but this emission seemed more madly exciting than any she had ever felt before, and was produced without the usual means. At length she fell asleep again, but dreamt continually of her brother.

He, for his part, was mentally exercising a power he had acquired in Germany (the peculiar circumstance of the manner in which he gained this knowledge will be duly explained later on), and this was sufficient to account for his sister's condition.

Punctually at six o'clock on the following morning, brother and sister met in the hall. She threw herself into his arms and embraced him with great affection. "You darling brother," said she, "how glad I am to have you back with us; it seems like a new world to me."

"My dearest sister," replied he, "it is I who am the happy one, I cannot express to you the delight and happiness I feel in your society, after so long an absence."

After embracing again they started on their ramble; Ethel pointed out all her pet flowers and every spot that she liked, until they found themselves, at length, in a charming little grove overhanging the beach.

"Frank, darling," said she, "I have a headache; shall we sit down here and rest a short time until it goes away?"

"Certainly, my darling, and I think I can relieve that headache by a simple expedient I learned in Germany."

He then sat down opposite to her, and taking her two thumbs held them in the palm of his left hand, while with the right he made passes from her head to her feet, at the same time gazing into her eyes with a literally devouring look.

As he proceeded the humidity in her lovely eyes increased until the eyelids at last closed, and her head sank on her bosom.

After continuing the passes for a short time longer, her brother, still keeping his eyes fixed on her, gradually allowed her hands to slip away from his, and fall on her lap. He appeared intensely excited, his nostrils were dilated, he breathed hard, and his eyes seemed to burn in their sockets.

He gently laid Ethel down on her back, and after waiting to satisfy himself that she was in a fast mesmeric sleep, he placed one throbbing hand on her hip, and gradually raising it till he found the lovely prominence of one charming bosom, then his other hand sought its companion, and he pressed those heaving hills of snow which he felt perfectly under her thin muslin dress. He next knelt down by her side, and brought her breasts fully to view; they were indeed lovely, the two little pink nipples were stiffly erected, and seemed wooing to be kissed. She wore no stays, and his hand wandered over her lovely velvety skin down to her enchanting belly. Then rising, he leant forwards and gradually raised her dress in front.

First, her lovely ankles were seen, then her swelling calves, beautifully shaped knees, and glorious thighs. Frank felt faint and sick, and was compelled to desist from further exploration till he had somewhat recovered.

In a few moments he gently separated those divine thighs, and his eyes were riveted on his sister's darling little cunt, which now lay fully exposed to view. Two lovely coral lips, which were slightly parted, moist and throbbing, first met his gaze. He separated them yet further with his finger and saw the exquisite clitoris perfectly visible. Utterly unable to resist the temptation, he glued his lips to the lovely spot, and titillated the clitoris with his tongue. Almost immediately she began to writhe and twist about, and he felt her balmy emission flow into his mouth as she spent with low moans. He then desisted, and releasing his bursting prick commenced slowly to frig himself, while gazing on the exquisite beauties exhibited to his view. With spasmodic jerks the semen flew from him while he moaned with pleasure.

Now fearing discovery, he carefully wiped his sister's cunt with his handkerchief, which he madly kissed afterwards, and adjusted her dress, removed all traces of his own spending, and proceeded to awaken his sister. Placing her in a sitting position against a tree, he recommenced his passes, this time in a contrary direction, and she soon after opened her eyes.

After looking at him vaguely for a moment, she flung her arms round his neck, and kissed him. "Oh," she said, "I have been asleep, and had such a delicious dream."

"Has your headache gone?" said he.

"Oh," she replied, "I did have a headache, but not a symptom of it remains."

She was evidently utterly unconscious of all that had taken place, and her brother suggested they should resume their walk.

At breakfast Mrs. Etheridge said, "You have had a walk betimes this morning, my children, and you are both looking quite rosy."

So they were, but she little knew the cause.

After breakfast Mr. Etheridge addressed himself to his son, "Your mamma and myself are obliged to go to Lynton this afternoon on family business, and I fear we shall not be able to return until late, but I have no doubt you will be able to amuse yourself; Ethel will, I am sure, do her best to keep you from getting dull on your first arrival at home, after so long an absence."

When they had started, Frank accompanied Ethel into her sitting room, and begged her to sing and play for him, in order that he might hear what progress she had made.

She at once complied with his request, and he sat by her side watching with glaring eye the rise and fall of her lovely bosom as she sang him a charming little song, full of simple natural tenderness. He was, in fact, lusting madly for his own sister, and why not?

In the earliest history of our own race incest was no sin; why should we now consider it as such? On the other hand what can be more intensely exciting than the knowledge that one is indulging every feeling of lasciviousness conjointly with one united so nearly by ties of blood and kindred.

When she had finished he burned to enjoy her, but dared not, and with an effort he left the room, saying that he had some letters to write.

He went to his bedroom, but on his way thither he saw the adjoining door open and recognized a dress his sister had worn on the previous evening hanging against the wall. Her bed was still unmade, her nightdress was lying on it, and by the side of the bed a pair of drawers that she left there on changing her underlinen. He rushed to the bed, kissed the nightdress, and literally glued his lips to that portion of her drawers which had covered her darling little cunt. He was so excited that he could scarcely forbear from spending on the spot. Hearing approaching footsteps he immediately made his way to his own room, and bolting the door, he tore off his trousers. Doubling up the pillow, he inserted his erect prick between the folds, and straining it tightly between his thighs, threw himself forward on the bed, and thinking of his darling sister, with a few heaves backwards and forwards, spent deliciously. He then lay down and pondered over the best means of attaining his desires, for he resolved that he would enjoy his sister in every conceivable manner, let the consequences be what they might.

His meditations were interrupted by the luncheon bell. He descended to the dining room, and the sight of his sister aroused his desires with redoubled force; he devoured her with his eyes, and she again exhibited the same restless and uncomfortable symptoms that possessed her in the morning; her colour rose, her bosom rose and fell tumultuously, she squeezed her thighs together, sighed deeply, and seemed altogether unlike herself.

Seeing this he averted his gaze, and commenced talking on indifferent subjects. When the servants had left the room, he suggested another stroll on the grounds, as it was such a lovely afternoon. She consented with delight, and they set forth.

After rambling some distance from the house, she said, "Frank, my darling, there is such a lovely summer house in this thicket where I often come and read, shall we go in and rest?"

Frank was delighted at the idea. It was a charming little retreat, completely hidden by trees, and furnished most luxuriously—a velvet couch, an easy chair, and a lounge occupying the whole of one side invited to repose.

They sat down, and Frank's arm wound round his sister's enticing waist, and he could not resist kissing those lovely pouting lips. She trembled like an aspen, and as he gazed into her moist and humid eyes, the strange symptoms reappeared.

Frank could no longer resist, but holding her thumbs he commenced the magnetic passes, and she speedily fell into his arms, apparently in a deep slumber. He now sought to see if he was entirely successful in his attempt to produce the effect he desired, and therefore taking her in his arms and laying her on the couch, he said, "Ethel, do you know where you are?"

"With my darling brother," she replied.

"Do you love him?"

"Madly," was the reply.

"What would you like to do to prove that love?"

"Anything he desires."

"Stand up."

She did so.

"Unfasten your dress; take it off."

She complied immediately.

"Loosen your petticoats and take them off; now your slippers and your stockings."

The dear girl did exactly as requested, still in the same dreamy, languid manner. She now stood in her chemise and drawers only, and Frank felt as if he would faint. This splendid girl standing before him; lovely ankles, calves, and bare feet and those enchanting breasts peeping over her embroidered chemise, constituted a most voluptuous sight.

"Now, my darling," said he, "remove your drawers."

She did so, and he snatched them up and covered them with kisses.

"Now the chemise."

That also was taken off with alacrity, and she was before him perfectly naked. Heavens! What a sight! The whiteness of her skin, which shone like alabaster, the exquisite contour of her limbs, and the tremulous motion which pervaded every muscle, formed a combination of lustful excitement that utterly baffles description.

He then ordered her to lie down on her back, raise her knees, and place her heels against her buttocks, then insert her finger in that divine cunt and frig herself.

She did so.

"How do you feel, darling? Are you going to spend? I will that you spend at once."

Her whole body stiffened.

"Keep your thighs widely extended," he said, "so that I can see every throb that convulses your cunt, when the lovely liquor of love oozes forth."

She obeyed, and with a deep sigh he saw it gush forth and cover her caressing hand.

He rushed forward and gamahuched her furiously, and then sitting in an easy chair, said, "Ethel, get up."

She obeyed, and following his commands, knelt in front of him, unfastened the front of his trousers, inserted her hand, and drew forth his prick; she then sucked it until with a positive howl of delight he inundated her mouth with his spendings. He then desired her to rise and kneel on the couch, then coming behind her he gently pulled apart the cheeks of her divine bottom, and disclosed the little orifice that lay nestling between them. This he sucked till he spent again, clasping her hips as he spent with spasmodic force.

He burned to fuck her, but dared not venture, and after a short time he ordered her to resume her clothes, and then repeated the passes in a contrary direction until she recovered her senses, and to his great delight, she evidently knew nothing of what had taken place.

Mr. and Mrs. Etheridge had not returned when they reached the house, and they found a note stating that they were detained and could not be home till the following day.

On reading this Frank immediately remembered the proximity of his sister's bedroom and determined, at any risk, to gratify his intense desire with respect to her, this very night.

Before retiring he embraced her warmly, pressing her breasts against his chest and pushing his belly against hers; to his intense delight he felt her whole frame vibrate from the intensity of her emotion as her head fell on his shoulder.

He bade her good night and departed to his room.

As soon as he was convinced the house was quiet he gently opened his door and stole on tiptoe to his sister's room. To his intense delight it was unfastened.

He entered and saw his sister lying on her snowy bed, which was illumined by the rays of the moon.

She slept; he watched for some moments the rise and fall of her bosom, and the exquisite beauty of her face, and then commenced to mesmerize her again. She moaned faintly, and appeared restless.

"Sleep," said he, and she immediately became quiet.

"Ethel," he continued, "do you know who is speaking to you?"

"Yes, my darling brother."

He next pulled down the bed-clothes, and gently placed himself by her side, naked as he was.

"My darling," said he, "take off your night dress and chemise."

She raised herself in the bed and did so, and then lay down again.

He clasped her in his arms, utterly intoxicated with his anticipated bliss.

The contact of her skin with his own, the knowledge that she was unconscious of what he was doing, and that it was his own sister, almost maddened him.

He was literally consumed with lust, and embraced her in every direction. Passing his arms between her thighs, he nestled his head on her divine belly. He next shifted it to her bosom, then he placed his prick between those firm and pouting breasts, then between her thighs. He next placed his finger inside the lips of her cunt, and found to his surprise that it entered easily.

"Thank God," he muttered, "she has been frigged, possibly fucked, and I shall not hurt her."

He willed her to take his prick and insert it in that divine recess, and to his intense joy he succeeded in burying himself in her with scarcely any difficulty.

He then lay powerless, and the spasm overtook him and ebbed forth into the inmost recesses of his sister's cunt.

He lay for a few moments in a profound lethargy, when he suddenly found his sister's cunt contracting and throbbing around his prick, which was still soaking within her. This fired him anew, and placing both hands beneath her buttocks, he pressed her cunt towards him with the utmost force, while driving in and out of her with deep and body-killing thrusts. They both spent simultaneously, and after a short pause he arose and contemplated her, then willing her to resume her night dress and chemise, he returned to his own room, fearing that he might fall asleep and be discovered in the morning.

As he lay down he noticed a ray of light in a dark corner of his room, and on examining the panelling, found that a crevice existed through which he could see perfectly into his sister's room. There she still lay slumbering peacefully, and it suddenly struck him that he had forgotten to awaken her from the magnetic sleep which evidently still overpowered her.

He immediately commenced the necessary process and, to his delight, found that it had the same effect, notwithstanding the wall which intervened.

She rose in the bed, and altering her position, lay calmly and naturally.

He retired to bed again, but was restless and excited and could not sleep; his prick was still stiff, and every nerve throbbed.

He lay tossing about in this way for an hour or so, when he suddenly heard a sound of whispering in the next room, and on peeping through the crevice into his sister's apartment, beheld a sight that rendered him spellbound and breathless.

He saw on her bed a figure perfectly naked, and of the most exquisite form, rivalling that of Ethel herself. She was kneeling and in the act of pulling the clothes from his sister, and raising her night dress, gazed ardently at her cunt. "How wet and sticky it is to-night, Miss. You must have had such a wet dream."

The lovely stranger placed her fingers within it and rubbed them about in the moisture, and then substituted her tongue, sucking luxuriously the lips and clitoris, and thrusting in the velvet tip as far as it would go into the vagina, until Ethel murmured, "It is coming again, Mabel. Oh! Oh! Suck harder, my dear." He now recognised the stranger as a housemaid who had attracted his attention on more than one occasion during the short time he had been in the house.

His sister now sought Mabel's cunt, and inserting a finger, commenced pushing it backwards and forwards as she embraced her lovely buttocks with her disengaged arm, burying her tongue within the rosy bottom-hole.

They writhed like two serpents, their bodies arched, and then they fell prone on each other, every muscle vibrating as they spent in all the agonies of lasciviousness.

Frank seized his prick and frigged himself in unison with their movements, spouting out a torrent of sperm at the same moment as the two lovely tribades lost consciousness in their blissful convulsions.

When he looked again Ethel had taken the housemaid across her knees, and was rubbing her belly and sucking her nipples, ever and anon allowing her hand to wander between her thighs. She then turned her with her belly downwards, so that their cunts were in contact, and again passing her hand between Mabel's thighs, she rubbed the profuse spendings with which their cunts overflowed into her exposed bottom-hole, and then inserting her finger, pushed it in and out its entire length, whilst Mable struggled to release herself.

At length she succeeded, and the housemaid lay flat on her back with Ethel reversed above her, and the sound of their mutual sucking, as their heads were between each other's thighs, drove Frank almost to the verge of distraction.

They swayed to and fro, and pressed each other with their utmost strength, until it was evident they were spending again. Still the gamahuching continued, until they seemed utterly exhausted; and Mabel, kissing Ethel madly, left the room, evidently to return to her own before the other servants were stirring, as the day was already breaking.

Frank was utterly bewildered, but now determined that he would use his knowledge and ravish his darling sister without the aid of mesmerism before many days had passed.

Mr. and Mrs. Etheridge returned about midday, and Frank was again struck by his mother's rare beauty and the fullness of her magnificent bosom. He looked at her fixedly, and, strange to say, she seemed affected by his gaze much in the same manner as his sister had been at first.

Frank felt a thrill of delight as the bare possibility occurred to him of revelling in his mother's charms, but he felt that if he ever did succeed the utmost caution would be necessary.

In the afternoon he took another stroll with his sister, and they soon found themselves in the summer house.

They sat side by side on the couch, and Frank warmly embraced her, pressing her to him with voluptuous energy. She looked into his eyes and breathed heavily. His hand roved down and pressed one cheek of her buttocks, which he felt undulate beneath her bottom.

"You must not do that," she murmured, "it makes me feel sick and ill."

"Does it when Mabel does the same?" asked Frank.

She became white with terror.

"Do not fear, my darling," continued Frank. "I know all, have seen your embraces last night, but alluded to it to assure you your secret is safe. But will you not now allow me some little privileges?"

"Oh, my darling, you are my brother!"

"So much greater the exquisite enjoyment," pleaded Frank.

Her head fell on his shoulder, and he ventured to insinuate his fingers within the bosom of her dress and gently rubbed her nipples with his thumb and finger.

She shivered with delight.

He next proceeded to place her hand upon his trousers, so that she could feel his bursting prick beneath. She clutched it wildly. He now gently pushed her backwards and placed one hand beneath her clothes, gently pressing her legs and thighs apart, until he at length succeeded in reaching her cunt, which was in a moist and spending condition.

She tore open his trousers, saying, "Oh! Darling, forgive me, I cannot help it," and pushed the skin of his prick backwards and forwards.

Frank commenced to frig her, at first gently, gradually increasing the rapidity and depth of his insertion, till, with a shriek of rapture, she spent profusely. He resisted the impulse to follow her example, and seating himself in a chair, drew her towards him, placed his knees between her thighs, and allowed her gradually to sit down, while his prick penetrated her.

They embraced madly, thrusting their tongues into each other's mouths, and even biting each other in the fury of their transports, until another emission relieved their feverish lubricity.

They then resumed their position on the couch, and Ethel burst into a flood of tears.

"Oh! My brother," sobbed she, "what have we done, and what will be the consequence?"

Frank strove to console her, and after a time succeeded, and she became calm, so that they could resume their walk and return to the house.

It is now time that some explanation should be offered as to the cause of the mesmeric power and voluptuous development so strikingly manifested in Frank.

When he first reached school in Germany he

was perfectly innocent, but was speedily initiated into all the mysteries of frigging and prick sucking by his school-fellows, who also used to fuck each other between the thighs, while a third behind received the point of his prick in his mouth each time it was pressed forward and sucked out every drop of spend that he could obtain.

One day when passing one of the master's rooms, he peeped in and saw him making mysterious motions in front of a pale, sickly boy, who was celebrated amongst his companions for the enormous size of his prick and balls.

He watched with curiosity, and saw the boy fall apparently asleep. The master then proceeded to divest him of his trousers, handling with evident delight the boy's private parts. He then tucked up his shirt under his waistcoat, leaving the whole of his belly, bottom, thighs, and his lovely prick exposed.

The master gazed with rapture, and Frank saw by the lump that suddenly appeared in his trousers that his cock was evidently standing erect and hard.

He then said. "Kneel on that sofa, and lean your arms on the head of it, I will it!"

Frank was intensely surprised to see the boy obey as though he were walking in his sleep.

The master took from an adjacent cupboard a birch and went to the head of the sofa, then leaning over the prostrate form of the boy commenced to flog him with it on his bottom and the inside of his thighs, but not severely.

He next unbuttoned his own trousers, and out

the boy seemed to have been rendered insensible, and the fact of a great prick perforating a bottom-hole also filled him with astonishment.

He resolved to make the attempt to achieve this latter result with this very boy, who slept in his dormitory, and try what it was like. And it may be added that he successfully carried his project into effect the same evening, to the great surprise and extreme delight of the boy, who had knowingly been operated on in a similar manner, probably on many occasions.

Shortly after this he spoke of the extraordinary power one being seemed to possess over another, making them unconscious, and then compelling them to obey their orders.

This was to a young student at a neighbouring college, with whom he had become intimate, even to the extent of frigging each other. This friend explained the theory and practice of mesmerism, and Frank soon found that he could also experimentalize successfully.

This young student was also an ardent voluptuary of the most pronounced type, and proposed that Frank should try if he could mesmerize his sister, a charming girl of about fifteen, who was staying with him for a few days, awaiting the arrival of her father. Frank's friend proposed they should go to a certain house, where he was in the habit of going, to try the experiment. It was, in fact, kept by a lady who allowed the strangest scenes of unbridled lust to be enacted there, the contemplation of which caused her the most exquisite delight.

They started at once, in company with his friend's sister, and on their arrival the lady ushered them into her drawing room (fully understanding that their visit was to afford her some of the usual voluptuous treats, which she always enjoyed so much), and Frank at once commenced to try his experiment on the Fräulein.

For some time no visible effect was produced, but at last her eyes appeared to dilate, then the eyelids drooped, and she seemed to sleep.

"Now, Frank," said his friend, "speak to her."

He did so, and to his delight he found that he had succeeded perfectly.

The student now told Frank that he must see him fuck her.

He started in amazement.

"Why she has never been touched! And I have never seen her cunt!"

"So much the better sport," replied his friend, "for I am determined you shall defile her in my presence here.

"Now, Frank," continued he, placing his hand on his prick and commencing to fondle it, "no one but ourselves can ever know anything about it. I am so anxious to see her naked body, and this darling prick penetrating it. I see you will," said he as he felt the cock rising under his caressing hand.

Frank was ready for anything. He approached her, unfastened her dress, discovered her rosy nipples tipping the snowy hills of her bosom. He fingered them in rapture, and they seemed to get so impudently hard that he could not resist the

temptation of sucking the delicious little straw-
berries of love. But, his friend getting impatient,
he proceeded to raise her dress in front, exhibiting
a lovely little pink cunt, with scarcely a hair on it.

"I will assist you to undress her," said the
brother, and lifting her on the couch she was soon
naked in their hands.

Frank examined that deliciously tight little
cunt; it was impossible to get even the point of his
finger in.

"How can I fuck this?" said he.

"Nonsense!" said the brother. "Suck it and
moisten it."

Frank did so, and from the writhing of the
naked body of the beautiful girl, she was evidently
enjoying it. Her brother then took his place and
endeavored to force his tongue within. At last he
arose, and said, "Frank, I fear you must place your
prick between her thighs and spend there, she is
so small and tight, and I will suck the head of
your prick from the other side."

This was carried into effect, and after commanding her to dress, Frank succeeded in recovering her
again, and they left the house.

This little incident had created in Frank's mind
a mad desire to force his way into a virgin cunt,
he revelling in the agony of his victim by anticipa-
tion, and on mentioning his desire to his friend,
he said, "I will speak to a lady that I know very
well."

This was the proprietress of the house they had
visited with his sister. She had a girl of eighteen of

French parentage who had been turned out of her home by brutal parents and was, in fact, utterly friendless.

Madame G—— had taken her in with delight, seeing that she would be able to do anything with her that her lewd fancies might devise, without fear or risk.

This was the victim fated to be tortured by Frank, the only condition being that Madame G—— should be present to see the whole proceeding, and thus have her share of the voluptuous feast.

On the following day Frank obtained permission to be absent until evening, and he accompanied his friend to the house in question.

They were ushered into a charming boudoir, where they found Madame G—— awaiting them. She was a pretty, plump woman, every feature betraying an intensely lascivious temperament. She was completely enveloped in a dressing gown of black velvet, which heightened the dazzling whiteness of her skin; her rosy little feet were encased in tiny little slippers, and her legs were evidently bare.

A soft warm air pervaded the room, and a fragrant and exciting perfume shed its influence around. The floor was covered with a thick velvet pile carpet; the chairs and a capacious couch were also covered with velvet and furnished with luxurious springs. In the centre of the room was a peculiar article of furniture, which bore the appearance of a St. Andrew's Cross, placed horizontally and supported by a massive pedestal, which at one end was cut away so as to correspond with the form of the cross at its lower extremity.

She rose and greeted them, embracing both most affectionately, and squeezed Frank so ardently against her that his prick stood immediately. Finding this to be the case she took his hand and placed it beneath her dressing gown; he shuddered on discovering that it was the only article that concealed her nakedness.

He pressed her belly amorously, and placing his hand at the junction of her thighs, discovered a most exquisite cunt and a clitoris erect and hard. She would not allow him to proceed further, as she only wished to see if he was sufficiently excited for the work he was intended to perform.

All sitting down, they partook of some Burgundy and literally devoured a collection of books, photographs, and pictures she placed before them. They were of the most fearfully exciting character, representing lust and cruelty in every phase; the principal works being the Marquis de Sade's *Justine* and *Juliette,* in ten volumes, with their one hundred steel plates, also his *Philosophie dans le Boudoir* and other French works, besides English erotic books, such as *Fanny Hill, The Romance of Lust, Letters from Paris, Curiosities of Flagellation, Phoebe Kissagen, The New Epicurean,* and others too numerous to be mentioned.

When she saw they were both half frantic, she rose and rang the bell. In a few moments the door opened, and a remarkably beautiful girl entered.

"Sit down," said Madame G———, "I wish to speak to you."

She obeyed, evidently frightened at the sight of two strange young gentlemen.

Madame then locked the door, and placing the key on the mantelpiece, turned to their victim.

"Marie," said she, addressing the girl, "these two handsome young fellows are going to fuck you. Do you know what that means?"

The poor girl began to sob, and trembled from head to foot.

"Oh! Madame," said she, "have mercy! I am so terrified—pray let me go!"

"No," thundered her tormentor, "I will not. Your screams cannot be heard beyond this room, and I intend to gloat over your agonies, while you are tortured by all here. Seize her," she added, addressing Frank and his friend, who were evidently influenced by the same feelings of ungovernable lust.

They sprang up and held her fast.

"Undress her."

This they endeavored to do, but her struggles were such that they could not succeed.

Madame G—— now approached, and seizing her arms, held them as in a vise, and directed Frank's friend to hold her legs. Frank then tore open her dress, and throwing her on the floor, they succeeded by their joint endeavours in tearing it completely off. She was forcibly divested of her stays, petticoats, drawers, stockings, everything in fact, till at last she lay on the floor struggling and screaming in a perfectly nude condition.

"Lift her on the cross table," said Madame.

And with some difficulty they succeeded in extending their victim on her back, with her legs and arms stretched out on the four branches of the cross, and securely fixed in that position by concealed springs.

There lay her lovely naked form, every muscle convulsed by fear and outraged modesty.

Madame G—— then proceeded to suck her breasts and rub her belly and the inside of her thighs, directing Frank to fondle her cunt. This he obeyed delightedly, and then proceeded to suck it, causing her to struggle more and more, as in spite of all her fear and the shock to her modesty she was becoming excited, and in a few moments gave down a most copious spend.

This was the signal Madame was waiting for. "Now," she exclaimed, "your maidenhead shall be broken through—lost and destroyed!"

Frank and his friend stripped themselves to the buff, Madame also throwing off her only garment.

Acting on her instructions, Frank approached the lower end of the cross table, and placing himself between the victim's legs, placed the point of his prick just within the lips of her spending cunt, his friend taking up his station at the other end of the table with his rampant fiery cock just above the horrified face.

Madame, for her part, knelt on a prie-dieu, from the back of which protruded a dildo, which immediately entered her ready cunt to the very hilt, and leaning forward she recommended sucking and biting the tender nipples of her victim.

Frank now gave a brutal lunge, and excited to madness by the shrieks of agony and helpless struggles of the poor girl, was buried in her in a moment, his ruthless prick breaking or tearing through every maiden obstacle, till the virgin blood trickled over his testicles and down the crack of her bottom.

His friend now commenced to frig himself, and Madame G—— was also pushing furiously backwards and forwards on the dildo, as Frank now fucked the girl with deep and agonizing insertions of his prick.

The victim fainted from excess of pain and emotion, seeing which, Madame violently bit her bosom, and she recovered consciousness with a shriek of anguish, just as Frank spent within her lacerated body, and his friend inundated her face with the spunk that poured from his spending prick. At the same time Madame covered her dildo also with a prolific emission. This only increased the frenzy of her tormentors, and springing to their feet they eagerly agreed to Madame's suggestion to flog her.

Having reversed their victim so that she now lay on her belly, with a concealed dildo of immense size forcing itself up her cunt, they proceeded with three immense birch rods to carry this into effect, lashing her bottom, loins, inside her thighs, and even the lips of her cunt, tightly distended around the hugh dildo, till the hue of her skin was a burning scarlet.

Then desisting, Madame G—— took another dildo, and pulling wider apart the cheeks of that smarting bottom, thrust it into her convulsed and agonized bottom-hole with hellish force.

The victim's tortures were almost too great for human endurance.

"Now," Madame exclaimed, with the wild glare of a demoniac, "I will sit astraddle her waist, and Frank must do so also, facing me."

This was immediately carried into effect, Frank's prick entered the cunt in front of him with the greatest ease. Their violent up and down motions caused the dildo buried in the cunt of the almost crushed victim to fuck her.

"Faster, faster," shrieked Madame G———. "I'm coming—I'm coming—I'm spending!"

Their movements were fast and furious, and just as their spunk flowed with convulsive throbs, Frank's friend thrust two pins into the quivering buttocks of the victim, causing the most exquisite torture.

She moaned piteously, but this only excited her tormentors' devilish lusts to a greater extent, and joining each other on the couch, they enacted every device of lasciviousness, goaded by the spectacle of the suffering girl.

They sucked and frigged, spending over each other in every direction. Then getting up, Frank withdrew the dildo from the bottom-hole of the suffering girl, substituted his prick, which was slippery with spendings, and commenced to fuck her there, whilst his friend inserted his under one of her extended arms, so that the point rubbed against one of the nipples of her bosom.

Madame G———, not to be behind hand, again seated herself astraddle the victim's waist, and rubbing her opened cunt in the spendings that still remained on her back from the previous fucking that had taken place there, frigged herself thus, as Frank increased her excitement and pleasure by working his moistened finger in the wrinkled bumhole she presented to his view, to her intense enjoyment.

They all spent at the same time, even the victim, who could not resist the effect of the dildo still within her cunt. She was now literally inundated with spunk, and utterly exhausted, as the others resumed their clothes.

It can easily be imagined that this extraordinary adventure corrupted Frank Etheridge's mind, and his madly lascivious temperament is no longer a matter of surprise to the reader.

To return to our story. A few days after Frank and Ethel had knowingly fucked, Mr. and Mrs. Etheridge were obliged to visit London, and the brother and sister resolved to utilise the occasion.

Frank, during the interim, had succeeded in gamahuching and fucking the housemaid who had visited his sister in her room on that memorable night.

He had prevailed on his sister to have her as a bedfellow, and enact every species of exciting lust and tribadism they could devise.

This was carried into effect, and Frank, from his post of observation at the crevice, saw them perfectly naked, lying on the outside of the bed, the housemaid being reversed above her mistress, while they were literally devouring each other's cunts.

He then descended, and softly entering the room, naked as he was, made a sign to his sister. She instantly clutched the body of the housemaid above her, so that she could not extricate herself from the position she was in.

Frank now approached; and having previously applied oil plentifully to his prick, he knelt over his sister's face, and with a sudden thrust forward, buried it within the bottom-hole of the astonished housemaid.

She screamed in alarm, but Ethel, raising her thighs, literally buried the girl's head between them and effectually stifled her cries.

Frank proceeded to push his prick in and out, as he revelled in this charming aperture, while his sister, abandoning for a moment the delicious cunt she was sucking, took his slippery balls in her mouth and rolled her tongue around them in such an exciting manner that he spent immediately, his spunk oozing out and flowing over the face of his delighted sister.

Mabel also emitted at the same moment, so that Ethel was almost choked.

Mabel was now ready enough to join in whatever they wished, and every species of ingenuity conceivable was brought into requisition, in order to minister to their mutual gratification.

At last Frank retired to his own room, sleeping soundly till late in the morning, when he awoke with such an awful cockstand and such a feeling of insatiable lust that he could scarcely put his prick out of sight in his trousers and make a decent appearance at the breakfast table.

He easily persuaded his sister to join him in a warm bath, which Mabel was ordered to prepare at once, and then when they had entered it she was to lock herself in Ethel's bedroom so that the other servants might not by any accident discover what was taking place.

Entering the bath, they lay down side by side, and an exquisite feeling of languor overtook them.

Ethel's hand wandered over her brother's naked form beneath the water, and his was not idle.

Then rising, they stood facing each other, and slightly extending her thighs, her brother speedily placed his erect and throbbing prick within her. They commenced to fuck gently, fondling each other as they did so.

The convulsive spasms, however, speedily approached, and at the moment they mutually commenced to spend they sank down in the warm water. The beautiful warmth of the aromatic bath produced most delicious sensations flowing up their bottom-holes, as busy fingers worked excitedly to increase their lascivious abandon, while its action around their still more sensitive organs of generation caused them heavenly rapture.

The day before the return of their parents, Frank and Ethel were seated in the summer house mutually fondling each other's private parts, when Frank said that the desire he had long felt to see his mother's glorious nakedness, and if possible to fuck and gamahuche her, grew stronger every day, and he was resolved to try it by the aid of mesmerism.

Ethel, blushing deeply, was evidently much excited by the idea, and confessed that the same feeling with respect to her father had possessed her for some time.

"Then, my darling," continued her brother, "we will do it."

Mabel now entered, and stopped further conversation by frigging herself before them, while they also performed the same act for each other, after which they all returned to the house.

Mr. and Mrs. Etheridge arrived the next day about one o'clock. They embraced their children with great warmth, but little imagined the libidinous feelings their endearments produced on their children.

It will be well, before relating what subsequently took place, to glance at Ethel's school experiences, in order to understand her lustful desires and warm temperament.

The school in Paris at which she was placed was conducted by a lady of tall stature, Juno-like form, and a manner which, outwardly mild, concealed beneath it the fire of raging lust, which she gratified in a peculiar manner.

She received Ethel most kindly, and kissing her affectionately, consigned her to the care of a young lady some three or four years older, who would be her special companion and share her bed.

She was afterwards introduced to the other young ladies, and at once felt thoroughly at home.

When they retired for the night, Ethel's companion, Minette, insisted on helping her to undress, and although from a natural feeling of shyness Ethel did not like it much, she did not wish to appear ill-natured or ungrateful, so she permitted it.

Minette managed in this operation, apparently by accident, to bring her hands in contact with Ethel's naked body as much as possible, which caused blushes to mantle her face, as she felt the contact of the soft, pulpy hand.

Ethel now got into bed, having first rendered similar assistance to Minette, who did not possess the shyness of her younger friend, but before putting on her nightdress completely bared her whole body before the eyes of Ethel, who was somewhat surprised to see such large prominent breasts and a profusion of hair covering her cunt.

She immediately embraced Ethel on getting into bed and endeavored to interlace their legs, which somewhat surprised the new pupil, and made her keep them close together, not knowing the meaning of such proceedings.

Before sleeping they lay apart, and Ethel, tired out as she was, speedily sank into a refreshing slumber.

She dreamt that every portion of her body was pervaded by the most delicious sensations, but could not conceive the cause, and when she awoke in the morning was surprised to find one of Minette's hands between her thighs, whilst another rested on her little breasts.

Her companion was asleep, or pretended to be so, and was entirely uncovered, the bed-clothes having slipped off. She was lying on her back, her legs widely extended, and her cunt moist, slightly open and occasionally twitching with a spasmodic throb, whilst she sighed gently and smiled in her sleep.

Ethel was possessed by a nameless sensation, and actuated by curiosity, ventured to look closer at the full-blown cunt, which seemed to rivet her gaze, and saw a little fleshy lump protruding from between the luscious-looking vermillion lips.

Struck with amazement, as she herself had nothing of the kind, she touched it gently with her fingers. It throbbed, and Minette sighed slightly, and said, in a kind of subdued whisper, "Oh, do go on, rub your finger about, my darling Clara, it is so exquisite!"

She was evidently asleep, and imagined someone else was with her.

Ethel, hardly knowing what she was about, commenced to rub the little lump, and was surprised still more to find that Minette moved uneasily, opening and shutting her legs, till at last she heard a profound sigh, and Minette lay motionless.

Ethel felt a strange throbbing, and her finger was immediately wetted with a warm gush of thick creamy glutinous something which was emitted from the cunt of her bedfellow.

This so affected her that she withdrew her finger, and lay apart from her companion again.

Presently the sleeper awoke, and they dressed, Minette again insisting on various squeezings and fondlings, which now produced on Ethel a most strange effect, perfectly incomprehensible to her, whilst Minette seemed also intensely excited.

However, they descended to breakfast without any further adventure, except that another pupil, Mademoiselle Rosalie, a frolicsome blonde, handed Ethel on the sly a piece of poetry in English, which she pretended she could not read herself but which might perhaps interest "la belle Anglaise."

Ethel put the printed slip away in her bosom, and afterwards read at her leisure as follows, a very comical parody:

PITY THE SORROWS

(Parody on Pratt's "Pity the Sorrows of a Poor Old Man," Annual Register 1770, page 222)

Pity the sorrows of a fat young wife,
 Whose youth and vigour make her pine
  the more!
Whose bounding pulse with hot desire is rife,
 O give relief, and heaven shall bless your
  store!

These rosy cheeks, my bursting youth
  bespeak,
 These beaming eyes proclaim my ardent
  quim,
But O! my husband is so cold and weak,
 I might be dead, and buried too, for him!

My widow'd sister Mary pines like me,
 But while he liv'd, her husband was a man!
My married sister Lucy smiles to see,
 How oft I'm baffled since my hopes began!

I will not, cannot tell, for very shame,
 All that is wanting to the married state,

To be a wife in nothing but the name,
　Is a most wretched, miserable fate!

Though chaste in heart, and willing to be
　　chaste,
　　What virtue can withstand the waltz's
　　whirl?
Tom, Jack, or Harry's arm about my waist,
　　Belly to belly throbbing, boy with girl!

To sup on partridges and to drink champagne,
　Stirs my hot blood to fever's ardent glow,
And then the waltzing round and round
　　again,
　　Drives me quite mad! O what, what can
　　I do?

I'd willingly be wise and chaste, God knows!
　But O, it drives me wild with amorous
　　pain,
To feel the embracing arms of waltzing
　　beaux,
　　To meet the piercing glance of charming
　　men!

O, tell me, have I err'd? Impart the truth!
　My inmost heart is open to conviction,
Deeper, O deeper still, dear vigorous youth,
　O, give me every inch of thine erection!

Pity the sorrows of a fat young wife,
　All, all my sins are lying at your door,
Bestow on me the biggest joys in life,
　Oh, give relief, and heav'n shall bless your
　　store!

Our school-girl was more perplexed than ever by this effusion: what was that something always required by blooming young wives or widows so mysteriously hinted at in the lines as she read them over and over again to herself?

At the close of their morning studies Madame Cul addressed her pupils and stated that Mademoiselle Rosalie had not completed her French exercises to her satisfaction, and as she could not allow idleness and carelessness to exist in her establishment, she would be birched in the presence of the whole school after luncheon.

Ethel stared in amazement, but Minette lovingly placed her arm round her waist and whispered, "It is the custom here, but you will soon get used to it, and even enjoy the sight."

According, before the commencement of afternoon studies, Madame Cul entered the schoolroom, followed by two well-formed but muscular and strong housemaids, and when all were assembled, said, "Mademoiselle Rosalie, come here and take off everything except your chemise, shoes and stockings. The maids will assist you to do so."

The poor girl advanced tremblingly, for she had not long entered the establishment, and this was but her second birching.

When she was divested of her dress Madame Cul directed one of the housemaids to assist her in getting on the other one's back, where she was securely held by the hands, the servant acting as horse, having her firmly gripped by each wrist, whilst the other strong young woman was directed to hold the victim's legs well apart.

Ethel gazed as if fascinated by the pretty and luscious sight presented to her view; it was so exciting to see Rosalie, who was about sixteen, with an exquisitely fair complexion, her face flushed with shame, with deep blue eyes brimful of tears, just ready to run down the crimson cheeks, as Madame Cul raised first her skirts, which brought to view the poor girl's pretty legs, dressed in most interesting boots, white silk stockings, and delicately trimmed drawers.

The poor girl seemed to quiver all over with emotion, as she first sobbed and then cried for mercy in a most piteous broken voice, "Oh, Madame, do pray punish me in private as you did at first. Ah, no, no! I can't bear the shame of their all seeing my poor naked bottom."

"Silly girl, hold that whimpering noise, you deserve all this disgrace, did I not tell you how I would punish you before the whole school next time?" said Madame, evidently with some excitement, as she opened the girl's drawers behind, and pinned up the tail of her chemise with all the rest of the impedimenta round the victim's waist, till at last they had a very fair view of Rosalie's lovely little pink-lipped cunt, upon which the incipient growth of soft down was only just beginning to be perceptible, and another delightful item displayed to view was her tight wrinkled little bumhole, set in a frame of soft-tinted delicate brown, beautifully in contrast with the snowy whiteness of the well-developed buttocks.

Madame now raised the birch with which she was provided, and commenced to lash the bottom so invitingly exhibited, increasing the severity of her cuts as she went on. Then resting a little she seemed to watch with much satisfaction the wriggling of the fair penitent, the cheeks of whose bottom were a fiery red.

When she recommenced, the birching was directed to the inside of the victim's thighs, and even on the lips of that delicately pink little cunt, with light smart touches, evidently intended to inflame the parts rather than cut them up.

Rosalie, her dark eyes now full of sensuous humidity, her face burning scarlet, alternately sobbed and cried as she commenced afresh to struggle wildly, so that the servants with all their strength could scarcely hold the plunging victim.

Madame Cul stopped the punishment, and to Ethel's intense surprise, she saw Rosalie's bottom-hole open and shut, whilst the throbbing lips of her cunt emitted a thick, whitish-looking liquid, which oozed forth in spasmodic gushes.

"Enough! She spends, the lewd girl; it only shows the prurient ideas girls must have when my birching affects them in such a sensual manner. Fie for shame, Mademoiselle Rosalie, what have you done?" exclaimed Madame, as she sank into a chair and seemed ready to faint herself, whilst the humidity of her eyes seemed the very counterpart to that sensuous look in her victim.

Recovering herself in a few moments, she directed them to release Rosalie, and then left the room.

During this extraordinary scene Minette had placed her hand behind Ethel and squeezed the cheeks of her bottom, also endeavoring to force it between her thighs as well as she could, considering how the intervening dress hindered this operation. Nevertheless our innocent novice could not help opening her legs a little, and felt a strange indescribable sensation of pleasure.

The other girls were moving restlessly on their seats and, in fact, were using dildoes concealed under their drapery.

When Minette and Ethel retired for the night, the former complained of the heat, and suggested that they should sleep without any covering or night dresses, and by way of example got into bed in a state of perfect nudity.

Ethel, not wishing to be thought prudish or ill-natured, first extinguished the light, and then threw off her chemise. Joining her companion bedfellow also quite naked, they embraced each other warmly and Minette, placing her hand on Ethel's bottom, forced their cunts together. She trembled from head to foot, but when Minette asked her to squeeze her in a similar manner, she did so at once, and did not resist the insertion of one of her fair thighs between her own.

Minette now kissed her furiously, thrusting her tongue into Ethel's mouth, causing her to feel the most extraordinary sensations.

"Ethel, my darling," she said, "what did you think of Rosalie's birching, has she not got an exquisite bottom and pussy? Was it not awfully exciting when it throbbed?"

At the same time she gently placed her hand on Ethel's cunt, and commenced to suck one of her nipples, whilst one finger was titillating her companion's incipient clitoris, which, although so small as to be scarcely visible, was tremendously sensitive to these tender and lascivious touches by such an experienced tribade.

"Oh, oh, pray don't, you make me feel so sick —so odd—I tremble all over—I can't say how I feel—and yet—yet—," said Ethel in a whisper, hardly knowing what to do as she struggled to get away a little from her rude bedfellow.

This only excited Minette the more, as she held the young girl firmly in her embrace, redoubling her ardent caresses, which seemed to send such a thrill of exquisite warmth through Ethel's entire frame that she was powerless to resist such seducing endearments.

Minette was not slow to take advantage of her conquest. Reversing her position all of a sudden, she forced her head between Ethel's thighs and commenced to suck her cunt, plunging her amorous velvety-tipped tongue in as far as it would go, or biting the little clitoris in such a way that her companion was almost mad with a feeling she could not yet fully understand.

She again struggled to release herself, but it was in reality only a semblance of resistance—the last faint protest of her modest nature before thoroughly surrendering herself to all the voluptuous games of Minette.

At last her head fell back, her throbbing cunt was raised to meet those warm, loving kisses, and then for the first time in her life, she really spent —and fainted.

When she recovered she threw herself into Minette's arms, saying, "Oh, I have indeed been in heaven. What did you do to make me feel so?"

Her bedfellow hastened to fondle her again, and before another hour had passed they were mutually frigging, gamahuching, and spending amid cries of delight. In fact, Ethel was thoroughly taught every pleasure possible to tribadism.

The following day another girl was birched in school, and at night Minette proposed to Ethel that they should go into the next dormitory, after the lights were extinguished, and see what was going on, as the birched girl slept there.

They did so, and Ethel stood spellbound.

Twelve girls, of ages varying from ten to sixteen, were all lying in a confused heap on two of the beds that had been placed close together, and they were sucking, frigging, and fucking each other with dildoes.

Minette rushed to the bed and speedily mingled with the spending mass of girlhood, whilst Ethel, utterly unable to resist the impulse, ran forward also to the birched girl and was soon sucking her cunt, whilst other girls sucked her nipples or excited her almost to madness by working their fingers in her sensitive bottom-hole. After exhausting themselves with every kind of lubricity, they returned to their own room.

The next morning Ethel felt so fatigued she could not complete the task assigned her in school.

As she was leaving for recreation Madame Cul called her to one side, and said: "You have incurred punishment by your neglect, but as you are evidently in a rather nervous state, I will inflict it in my bedroom. Come to me immediately after afternoon studies."

At the appointed time Ethel tremblingly sought Madame Cul's bedroom.

The schoolmistress, after locking the door, proceeded to assist her in removing all her clothes. When this was accomplished she directed her to lie on a velvet couch that was covered with cushions. This she did, and Madame Cul adjusted her in such a manner that while lying on her belly one of the velvet cushions lay between her extended thighs.

She now commenced to birch her with light stinging cuts that, although not apparently heavy enough to break or lacerate her delicate skin, had such a smarting effect that Ethel felt she must scream to relieve the pain. This was presently succeeded by a warm voluptuous glow that sent a tremor through her whole frame. She felt as though she wanted to pee, and yet that did not seem the reason of her strange sensations.

As the birching proceeded, Madame occasionally placed her hand on the bottom of the penitent, which tended so to increase Ethel's excitement that, wildly squeezing the cushion between her thighs, she spent copiously.

Madame, delighted to see what had happened, lifted her own skirts and with a few insertions of her finger produced the same result on herself.

When she had recovered she ordered Ethel to rise, then pretending to notice the moisture on the pillow, asked her what she had been doing.

Poor Ethel blushed scarlet, and looked awfully distressed.

"Come here, my darling," Madame said, "let me see what has been the matter with you," and she took her across her knees, extending her on her back.

She examined her cunt, pressed and rubbed her belly, squeezed her nipples beteen her fingers till they grew quite impudently erect, inserted her finger in Ethel's cunt, and commenced to frig the agitated girl luxuriously, making her toss about in such extasy that, when spending again, Madame could scarcely hold her, so violent were her contortions.

(Madame's finger entered easily, but she made no remark, for she knew full well that the entrance had been forced by Minette's finger—which was, in fact, the case.)

After this Ethel was initiated into every means of procuring sensual pleasure that Sapphism could teach, but it was not until her return home, and the subsequent meeting with her brother, that she actually felt the real delight of a prick inside her (which no substitutes can ever equal), although she knew all that man could do unto her.

It will be seen, therefore, that by reason of her school experiences she was well prepared for any species of lechery which her brother might venture to propose.

In the course of a few days Mr. Etheridge was compelled again to visit the neighbouring town where he would be detained till the next day.

Thus the opportunity came at last for which Frank had been waiting. At dinner he plied his mother with Burgundy (of which she was very fond) to the greatest possible extent, without raising her suspicions, whilst he literally devoured her with his gaze.

Later in the evening, she sat in a large easy chair and seemed to be getting drowsy. Frank said, "As we shall scarcely require anything else to-night, may the servants go to bed, Mamma?"

She assented, and after the order had been given, Frank, looking triumphantly towards his sister, seriously commenced his attempt to mesmerize his own mother. At first she involuntarily resisted his efforts, but at length she succumbed, and as her head fell on her shoulder he openly made the necessary passes, and she speedily became entirely at his mercy.

"Now, Ethel," said he, "I will gratify my passion."

He approached his mother. She was in evening dress and her lovely bubbies were half visible, and from the semirecumbent position in which she lay every outline of her form could be clearly seen.

Her son first carefully raised those deliciously firm bubbies completely above her dress, then sucking one motioned to his sister to do the same with the other.

Mrs. Etheridge sighed slightly and slid further down in her chair.

Frank then knelt in front of her, and his sister helping him, they gradually raised their Mamma's dress in front, till they had a full view of the splendid legs and thighs of their maternal parent—the former cased in pink silk stockings, with the swelling thighs filling out her drawers and making them look deliciously tight. Placing his hand within the slit in front he pulled aside the chemise, and gently extending her legs to their widest, he placed her feet on two chairs, and they now had a full view of that glorious cunt from which they both had come. It was beautifully shaded with hair, not too large, and between the moist lips he saw her divine clitoris, hard and erect.

After gazing for a moment, he rubbbed it gently with his finger. Mamma again sighed, and slid still further forwards. Now taking from his pocket a dildo (which he had previously charged), he gradually inserted it in his mother and pushed it gently backwards and forwards. The lips clung lovingly to it, his mother's breathing became hurried, her bubbies heaved under the caressing fingers of her daughter, and with a tremendous spasm that convulsed every muscle of her body, she spent, just as Frank pressed the spring and injected the contents of the dildo into her. Immediately removing the instrument and substituting his tongue, he drained every drop of spend that she emitted.

While he was thus occupied Ethel had stretched herself on the floor, and having released his bursting cock, was receiving within her mouth the spendings of her brother.

After gloating for some time over the sight of his mother's relaxed cunt, he suddenly placed her legs over his shoulders and raised her body in such a manner that his prick was opposite her bottom-hole. He, after his sister had rubbed some of the spunk within its wrinkled orifice, prepared for an *enculade*. Ethel meanwhile was gamahuching her mother's delicious cunt and being frigged by her brother.

Gradually Frank pushed his way within his Mamma's delightful fundament, which contracted and throbbed upon his tremendously excited prick, so that he at once spent in an agony of lust. His sister, equally maddened by the thoughts of her brother's incest and the voluptuous workings of his fingers on the lips of her cunt and clitoris, also emitted at the same time with a scream of rapture.

Then not to be outdone by her brother she made him withdraw his prick, which remained enormously stiff, and literally devoured it with her lips, sucking every drop of spend, etc., which still oozed from the fiery-looking head of his affair, and then pointing it to that divine maternal cunt she made him plunge in there and fuck Mamma properly and thoroughly, whilst she was sucking and tickling his balls in order to increase his enjoyment.

"Mamma, dear," said Frank, withdrawing his prick after another extatic spend, "do you know what you are doing?"

She answered immediately, "Yes, my darling children, your delicious fucking and gamahuching have made me feel all the delights of heaven itself."

Yet her eyes were closed, and there was no doubt of her being still under the mesmeric influence.

"Is there anything else you would like, dear Mother?" asked Frank.

"I should like to suck my dear boy's prick, whilst Ethel frigs me again," she murmured.

Frank at once presented his half-stiffened cock to his mother's lips, whilst Ethel, kneeling down between the maternal thighs, rolled her lascivious tongue in delight round that splendid clitoris and within the serrated nymphae which guarded the entrance to the temple of love, whilst her nose revelled amongst the beautiful *chevelure* of a most glorious *mons Veneris*, and inhaled all the sweet odours of that Cytherian region, which always has maddening effects on the votaries of gamahuching.

She was too occupied with her tongue to frig her mother's cunt, but postilioned her luxuriously with two fingers in her bottom-hole; Mamma all the while was sucking the prick and caressing the balls of her son, as he fucked her in the mouth.

At last they were too exhausted to carry their ideas any further for the time, and having wiped their mother and removed every trace of her defilement—and allowed a little time for the blood to cool in their veins—she was placed in her former position in her chair, her dress readjusted, and then Frank, with a few passes, brought her back to consciousness, after which they all soon retired to rest.

The following day at lunch time Mr. Etheridge returned home; but Mrs. Etheridge did not appear, having a severe headache, doubtless (although she knew it not) the result of the operations of her children on her body the previous evening.

It was a lovely afternoon, and Mr. Etheridge

proposed a walk, to which his children readily assented.

After strolling about for upwards of an hour they directed their steps to the summer house, of which mention has been before made.

Both Frank and Ethel had been more than usually affectionate in their manner to their father this particular afternoon, and the latter had more than once brushed accidentally with the back of her head against the front of her father's trousers, and on the last occasion distinctly felt his prick, which was evidently in a slightly turgid state, and his trousers also slightly projected in the most interesting place.

Ethel's breath shortened and her voice was slightly thick and husky with a strange tremulousness in its tone, as she felt a curious and unnatural sensation stealing over her that she could not define even in her own thoughts.

Frank also seemed strangely excited, and occasionally pressed his sister's bubbies behind his parent's back. He also took every opportunity of pressing against his father.

When they sat down to rest Ethel noticed that her father appeared drowsy, and he lay down on the couch. Presently his eyes closed, and he seemed in a deep sleep. On looking towards her brother she saw he was making the mesmeric passes with his hands.

In a few moments he rose, and approaching his sister, said, "My darling, Papa is now entirely unconscious of what he does, and entirely under my control; we will secure the door, and then you shall suck the author of your being till his noble prick spends in your mouth."

He appeared almost mad, and Ethel remained for the moment almost spellbound—her feelings were too much for her.

"Now, Ethel," continued her brother, "you can do what you wish, do not lose time!"

Aroused by his words, she approached her father and knelt down by the side of the couch. He was lying on his back, with his thighs slightly separated. Taking hold of his legs she gently extended them still further, and his prick could be seen reposing on his left thigh.

Ethel tremblingly unfastened the buttons from waist to fork; then, gently removing his shirt, she saw before her her father's lovely prick. It was an exquisite object, purely white, streaked with delicate blue veins, the loose skin almost covering the head of it. His balls were hanging gracefully beneath, and fine silky hair surrounded the whole of his privates.

She touched the prick, and even ventured to place her fingers round it; and as she did so its substance increased. She gently pushed the skin up and down, it throbbed and grew harder and stiffer every moment, till at last it was proudly erect, standing against his spotless belly, as white as ivory and as hard as a bar of iron.

She lay her cheek lovingly on his thigh and kissed the point of it, and then took it between her lips, while with her fingers she tickled his balls, which were now hard and tight in their receptacle.

Frank now knelt behind his sister, and having

raised her clothes, he seperated her legs and soon ascertained that her cunt was delightfully moist and hot. Bringing his prick to the mark, he slowly inserted it, and then pushed gently backwards and forwards.

His sister took more of the paternal priapus in her mouth, and pushing her head to and fro, frigged it deliciously by the double action of her lips and tongue. She grew more and more excited in her gamahuching as the motions of Frank's prick stirred all the lubricity of her nature, till suddenly Mr. Etheridge's lips parted with a deep-drawn sigh, the muscles of his belly hardened, and he spent in the mouth of his daughter, who also simultaneously received her brother's balmy emission in her cunt.

As the spending prick left the mouth of the gamahucher, Frank, withdrawing, took his sister in his arms, and thrusting his tongue into her mouth, they greedily enjoyed their father's spendings with which it was filled, as their hands mutually groped each other's prick and cunt.

Papa still lay on his back, his prick moist and glistening. Frank now seized the limp affair of his parent, and bringing his person close to his father, rubbed the head of the parental prick against that of his own. This immediately stiffened him again, and Frank directed Ethel to stand on the couch with her legs straddled over her father. She gradually stooped till the point of the great and glorious prick was at the entrance to her cunt, then with Frank's assistance it was guided into the lustful gap, she stooping lower and lower, till it penetrated her to the quick.

Her brother placed his hands under the cheeks of her bottom and jumped her up and down, till he saw by the contraction of his father's balls, and the immense increase of stiffness in the shaft of his prick, that he was about to spend again. Then he placed his head between his sister's thighs behind and with his tongue licked his father's balls and the lips of his sister's cunt, frigging himself at the same time.

When father and daughter spent, their joint spendings oozed out over his face and drove him frantic with enjoyment; then lifting his sister down, he made her suck his prick, which had just emitted, till it was stiff again, and then placing her on the floor he fucked her savagely, to her great delight in the excited state she then was, while he also frigged his father's cock till it came again in a copious spend.

They now removed all traces of what had happened; Frank then willed his father to awake, which he did. And looking round vacantly, he said, "Dear children, I fear I have been to sleep, the fresh air does tire me so," as he little thought of the real reason of his peculiar feelings of fatigue.

Frank, now perfectly sure that father, mother, and sister were entirely amenable to his influence, was determined to gratify his lusts to the full, and with the aid of Ethel he counted on carrying out his intentions.

In addition to gratifying their licentious appetites in the manner already related, they also sought new excitements by utilizing certain animals on the farm. Ethel would frig a bull or a goat, and when milking a favorite cow, would suddenly persuade Frank to lift her in his arms, where she would lay extended on her back, and raising her clothes, would frig herself with the cow's teats, the milk from which would flow into her ravenous cunt to be afterwards sucked out by her brother.

Frank would also stealthily approach a goat and raise the animal's hind legs; Ethel would put cold cream on its cunt for him and insert her brother's prick, who would then, utterly regardless of the cruelty he inflicted, force his cock in and spend there.

At last another idea occurred to them.

They were sitting after dinner when Frank quietly mesmerized both father and mother and then asked Ethel to dismiss the servants for the night.

They amused themselves by playing with their parents' private parts for awhile, and then Frank willed them to go to their bedroom. This they immediately did. Brother and sister left them for a short time, retiring to their own rooms, and returned quite naked.

Their parents now mechanically divested themselves of every article of clothing, in obedience to the will of their son, whilst Frank also willed the housemaid Maud to come into the room naked. This girl, under his influence, first approached Mrs. Etheridge and sucked her bubbies, then her cunt till she spent, after which she did the same with the prick of her master, while Frank and

Ethel gamahuched her bottom-hole and cunt to stimulate her lasciviousness; then she was sent back to her room.

Mr. and Mrs. Etheridge began to fondle, and after struggling a little together on the bed, Mamma was pulled onto her husband, and they commenced a most luscious St. George.

Heavens! What a sight for their incestuous son and daughter! With greedy eyes and bated breath, they watched that lovely prick appear and disappear within the loving cunt above it. Now the paroxysm of spending approached, and their voluptuous furor increased—it was simply maddening.

Frank and Ethel rushed forwards and with their hands assisted their beloved parents to experience the utmost possible enjoyment attainable, which they undoubtedly did, literally screaming with pleasure, as the spunk came forth in prolific streams.

Frank now determined to run a great risk in allowing his parents to know what was going on.

First directing his sister to lie on her back on the bed, with extended thighs, he willed his father to lie on her and himself placed his prick within her cunt. Then his mother (under his influence) lay on her back, on the bed by Ethel's side, and Frank, excitedly mounting upon her, buried his prick within the moist and juicy folds of the delicious cunt that gave him birth.

As they were all four approaching the divine climax, Frank dissolved the mesmeric charm and allowed both father and mother to realise the situation at a moment when it would be impossible for them to resist the impulses of their carnal nature.

Mr. Etheridge gave a cry of horror, and Mamma screamed with fright, but Ethel held her father in a convulsive embrace, her erotic fury making her at the moment as strong as a lioness, whilst Frank for his part thrust so vigorously at his mother that, in spite of their horror at the incestuous situation, they all spent simultaneously.

It would be impossible to describe the sense of shame that overcame the poor parents; they seemed to think they were still under the influence of some horrible dream, an idea which their children did their best to foster, whilst they were delighted by the sight of their father's fine prick stiffening again of itself, from the mere thought of having enjoyed his daughter.

Presently Ethel and her brother glided noiselessly from the room, but remained just outside the door to peep and listen. In a moment or two Mr. Etheridge threw himself upon his wife in a perfect transport of lust, exclaiming, "What a dream to fancy I've been fucking Ethel, and what joys she gave me! I feel, dear, as randy as if I had been away from you for six months!"

"How curious," sighed Mrs. Etheridge, "that I am also excited by having been dreaming the same thing about dear Frank! Ah, how fine, stiff, and hot your love of a prick is, my dear, and as moist as if you had really had the girl. Put it into me quick, love, and I'll fancy you really are Frank.

I'm excited enough to do the real thing at this moment!"

"For shame, wife," responded Mr. Etheridge, "it's an awful sin even to think about, and yet they do say the great Napoleon used to fuck his own sisters and aunts, and considered he had a right to enjoy himself as he pleased."

"Besides," continued Mrs. Etheridge, "there's the case of Lot and his daughters, and no doubt they were thought quite as respectable as ever by their acquaintances afterwards. In fact, they must have told about it for Moses to have known how to write the tale, and he could not have been very horrified at the incest, as he makes no mention of its being discontinued by Lot when he found it out. And then, you know, the ancient kings of Egypt always preferred to marry their mothers or sisters."

Further remarks were stopped by the necessities of their amorous combat, so brother and sister retired, fully satisfied that their parents would soon be as easy as themselves with regard to incestuous intercourse with their children.

Next day Mr. and Mrs. Etheridge appeared greatly distressed and hardly able to look Frank and Ethel in the face, but in the course of a few days this all wore off. Their equanimity returned, and whether owing to the mysterious influence of mesmerism or otherwise, they afterwards willingly enacted every species of licentiousness with their own children.

One day Frank and Ethel related to their parents their experiences at college and school. Mr. Etheridge was so inflamed at the tale of the professor sodomizing the boy with the big prick that he declared he should never rest until Frank had procured him the same pleasure.

"Let me see," he said, "if I can think of a handsome, finely developed youth, who we can invite here some day for you to experimentalize upon. Yes, there's young Harry Mortimer. He has got a fine looking lump in his trousers—a perfect Adonis —I've often longed to handle his cock."

"You old sinner," laughed his wife, "I always thought you a strictly moral man. And to think your ideas ever ran in such a beastly course. I, too, must confess, now Frank's mesmerism has made us all free with one another, how hard it has often been for me to retain my reputation as a chaste wife. Why there's Dr. Stroker, our rector, who has tried me dozens of times, and once actually showed me his fine tool when we were alone in the drawing room. What a beauty it was! I almost fainted with desire."

"Ah," said Ethel, "that's nothing to what he did with me, when I had to go to the rectory to prepare for confirmation. I was always alone with him. He used to laugh and tell me that religion was all humbug, he himself only followed and preached it as his trade, to get a good living. He would draw me on his lap, put his hands up my clothes, and tell me my cunny would soon have a crop of beautiful soft hair on it. And one day he threw me back and kissed my cunt till I fainted, and when I came round my clothes were up to my waist, and he was standing between my legs as they hung over the side of the sofa and frigging himself so as to spend all over my belly, and after all would not let me go home till I had kissed and handled his cock. That was just before you sent me off to Madame Cul's school and no doubt all helped to make Minette's touches so awfully exciting when she began to seduce me with her wanton games."

"We'll have a game with him, Frank, my boy!" exclaimed Mr. Etheridge. "My idea now is that we may all do what we like to enjoy ourselves, only damn all jealousy. I'm a regular Communist now! Well, when I ride out to-morrow I will call and ask Harry to spend an early day with you."

"Have you found anything worth reading to us yet, Frank?" asked his Mamma.

"Yes, a little bit about the quarrels of the goddesses in heaven. It is an old volume of the writings of the 'London Spy.' Here it is," said Frank, taking up a book:

POEM

A health Jove began to the best end of Juno,
By which they had often been "Junctus in
Uno,"
The bowl went about with much simp'ring
and winking,
Each God lick'd his lips, at the health he was
drinking;
Whilst Venus and Pallas look'd ready to rave,
That her Goddesship's scut should such
preference have;

The bowl being large, hoping the rather
Their amiable rumps might have swam
    altogether.
Thus both being vex'd, Venus swore by her
    power,
The nectar had something in't, made it drink
    sowre:
Which Pallas confirm'd by her shield and her
    sword,
And vow'd 'twas as musty besides as a
    T——d
But Juno perceiving 'twas out of ill-nature,
That Venus and Pallas abus'd the good
    creature,
Because to her Peacock, precedence was given,
As the best and finest fledg'd bird in the
    Heaven;
Insinuating under a wink and a snicker,
As if the good health had corrupted the
    liquor:
And finding they'd cast this reflection upon
    her,
In Juno 'twas justice to stand by her honour:
Who raising her bum from her seat in a
    passion,
To Venus and Pallas she made this oration:
"Pray Goddesses! What do you mean, I
    beseech it,
To basely reflect on my Tippet-de-wichet?
I know by your smiles, leering looks, and
    your winks,
And your items and jeers, you'd insinuate it
    stinks:

Dispraising the nectar, well knowing you
    meant,
That a health to my Tw———t gave the juice
    an ill scent.
Nay, laugh if you please, for I know I'm
    extreamly
To blame, thus to blurt out a word so
    unseemly.
But all know the proverb, wherein it is said,
That a What is a What, and a Spade is a
    Spade;
And now I'm provok'd, for a truth I may
    tell it,
Tho' as red as a fox, yet it smells like a vi'let.
By Jove I'll be judge, if I am not as sweet,
I may say, as a primrose, from head to my
    feet.
And he, you may swear, who's my husband
    and lover,
Has kist me, and felt me, and smelt me all
    over,
And if he can say an ill scent does arise,
From my ears, or my armpits, my c———t,
    or my thighs,
Like rotten old Cheshire, low Vervane or
    Ling,
And altho' I'm goddess, I'll hang in a string.
Your self, Lady Fair, that arose from the sea,
Sure will not presume to be fragrant as me:
The spark that has laid at your feet all his
    trophies,
Has smelt you sometimes strong as pickl'd
    anchovies:

But what if he has, were you ranker and
  older,
You'd be e'en good enough for a smith or a
  soldier."
These words put the Goddess of Love in a
  fire,
And make her look redder than Mars that
  was by her.
"My beauty," said Venus, "obtain'd the
  Gold Apple."
"Mine A———s Kiss," says Juno, "you shall
  have a couple.
I'd have you to know, Queen of Sluts, I
  defie you,
And all you can say, or the bully that's by
  you.
And as for that Tomboy that boasts she can
  wield,
In quarrels and brangles, her lance and her
  shield,
That never yet tasted the heavenly blessing,
But always lov'd fighting, much better than
  kissing:
I know she'd be glad to be ravish'd by force,
By some lusty God, that's as strong as a horse.
But who'd be so forward, unless he was tipsie,
To choose for a miss, such a masculine gipsie?
A termagant dowdy, a nasty old maid;
Who flights copulation, as if she was spay'd:
Which makes me believe, that under her
  bodice,
She wants the dear gem, that's the pride of a
  Goddess."

Now Pallas, enrag'd at so high a reflection,
Cry'd out, "I thank Jove, I am made in
  perfection,
And ev'ry thing have, from a hole to a hair,
Becoming the Goddess of Wisdom and War;
As Paris well knew, when he took a survey,
Of those parts where a Goddess's excellence
  lay;
Who strok'd it and smil'd, when my legs he
  had parted,
And peep'd till I thought his poor eyes would
  have started.
Then licking his lips, did aver to be true,
I was each way as full well accomplish'd as
  you.
Indeed, Madam Juno, I'll therefore be plain,
If ever I hear these reflections again:
I vow as a Goddess, and no mortal sinner,
I shall have no patience, but handle your
  pinner."
With that the Great Jupiter rose up in hot
  anger,
And looking on Pallas, was ready to bang
  her.
"Pox take ye," says he, "is your scolding a
  lecture,
That ought to be preach'd o'er a bowl of
  good nectar?
To drink we came hither, to sing and be civil;
As gods, to be merry, and not play the devil.
Why, mortals on earth, that live crowded in
  allies,

As laundresses, porters, poor strumpets and
  bullies;
When got o'er a gallon of belch, or a sneaker
Of punch, could not wrangle more over their
  liquor.
And you that are Goddesses, thus to be
  squabbling,
As if you were bred up to scow'ring and
  dabbling!
And all for a fig, or a fart, or a feather,
Or some silly thing that's as trivial as either!
For shame, my Fair Goddesses, bridle your
  passions,
And make not in heaven such filthy orations
About your bumfiddles; a very fine jest!
When the heavens all know, they but stink
  at the best.
Tho' ye think you much mend with your
  washes the matter,
And help the ill-scent with your orange
  flower water;
But when you've done all, 'tis but playing
  the fool,
And like stifling a T——d, in a cedar close
  stool:
Besides, Gods of judgment have often confest
That the natural scent without art is the
  best."
The Goddesses all, at these sayings, took
  snuff,
And rose from their seats in a damnable huff:
Their frowns and their blushes, they mingled
  together,

And went off in a passion, I do not know whither.

"Here's another fine burlesque poem I'll read, if you don't mind," continued Frank, "it's called 'Vulcan and Venus.' "

VULCAN AND VENUS

Says Vulcan to Venus, "Pray where have you been?"
"Abroad," cries the Goddess, "to see and be seen."
"I fear," says the blacksmith, "you lead an ill life,
Tho' a Goddess, I doubt you're a bitch of a wife."
"Why, how now," cries Venus, "altho' you're my spouse,
If you bitch me, you brute, have a care of your brows;
Why sure you don't think, I, the Goddess of Beauty,
By dint of ill language, will prove the more true t'ye;
Be civil, you'd best, or I vow by my placket,
I'll make the god Mars bastinado your jacket!"
"Are you there with your bears?" Smung replies to his Hussey.
"Does Mars still refresh your old Furbilo, does he;
I feel by my forehead a coat that is scarlet,
Of all kinds of baits, is the best for a harlot;

For beauty, I find, as 'tis commonly said,
Will nibble like fish at a rag that is red;
But Hussey, tell me any more of your Mars,
And I'll run a hot bar in your Goddesship's
  arse;
I fear not your threats, there's a fart for your
  bully,
No whore in the Heavens shall make me her
  cully!"
"You run a hot bar in my bum," quoth the
  dame,
"Its a sign you've a mighty respect for the
  same;
If your love be so little as to abuse it,
I'll keep it for those who know better to
  use it;
I'm certain no Goddess that values her
  honour,
Would bear the indignities you put upon her,
And not from that minute resolve out of
  spite,
To improve your old horns till they hang in
  your light."
"You're an impudent slut," cries the smung
  at his bellows,
"And I the unhappiest of all marry'd fellows:
I know you have made me a ram, I have
  seen it,
I catch'd you, you Whore, in the critical
  minute,
Fast lock'd in the arms of your lecherous
  God,

Whilst his brawny posteriors went niddity
   nod;
And you, like a Slut, lay as pleased and
   contented,
As if every joint of your body consented;
Altho' when you found you were spy'd by
   your buck,
Then you struggl'd and strove like a pig that
   is stuck,
And dismounting your God, would have
   made your escape,
But I saw by your actions it could be no
   rape;
Tho' when you first heard, by my patting-
   shoe tread,
My approach to your Whoreship's adulterous
   bed,
I know you'd have flown with your coats
   and your bodice,
And afterwards vow'd 'twas some other lewd
   Goddess;
But my net was too strong, it prevented your
   flying,
And so put a stop to your swearing and
   lying.
Besides, that the Gods might behold what a
   Slut
Of a Beautiful Queen they amongst them had
   got,
I call'd 'em about, that their Honours might
   stand,
And be pimps to your Goddesship's bus'ness
   in hand,

That in case you the truth shou'd hereafter
    deny,
I might call the whole Heavens to witness
    you lie.''
"And what did you get?" cries the amorous
    dame,
"For the pains that you took, but a Cuckoldy
    Name;
'Tis true you're confirmed you've a Whore
    for your wife,
Pray is that any comfort or ease to your life;
And have made it appear to the Gods as a
    jest,
That your wife's reputation is none of the
    best;
Does that make your labour more easy or
    sweet,
Or give you more gust to your drink or your
    meat?
'Tis true, you are fam'd for the net you have
    made,
Pray what did you catch in't but horns for
    your head;
You know that your rival don't value a trap,
Or a net, any more than a child or a clap;
A soldier is never asham'd of his vices,
But rather is proud of a Goddess's kisses;
And thinks it adds more to a hero's renown,
To subdue a fair lady than conquer a town;
Your spite must be therefore intended alone,
Against me, and that my little faults might
    be known;
Since 'tis as it is, I am very well pleas'd,

Your head shall be loaded, my tail shall be
    eas'd;
For since you have publish'd my shame and
    disgrace,
And have made me a jest to the heavenly race;
I'll be impudent now, and whenever I meet,
My dear favourite Mars, tho' it be in the
    street;
If a bulk be but near, I will never more dally,
He shall, if it pleases him, ay marry shall he;
Thus all you shall get by your open detection,
Of one silly error in female affection,
Is a wife that will cuckold you worse out of
    spite,
Now she's catch'd, than before she e're did for
    delight;
To punish thy head and heart, that very vice,
Which I us'd but in private whilst honour
    was nice;
I'll publickly now practice over and o'er,
Till thou'rt fain'd for a Cuckold and I for
    a Whore."
Cries Vulcan, "Could ever man think that a
    Goddess,
Admir'd for her charms by such numbers of
    noddies,
Should ever be curst with so rampant a tail,
That will wallow more love-sap, than I can
    do ale;
A pox on your rump, for I plainly see 'tis
As salt as your parents, Oceanus and Tethys.
But had I first known you had sprung from
    salt water,

The Devil for me, should have marry'd the
    daughter;
Besides, you are grown both so lustful and
    bold,
And for all your sweet looks, have a
    Billingsgate tongue,
That is fifty times worse than a fishwoman's
    hung.
If these be the plagues of a beautiful wife,
O ease me, Great Jove, of so cursed a life;
If La Pies divine, who inhabit the Heavens,
Will Whore on like mortals, at sixes and
    sevens;
Rave, rattle, and taunt at their horrify'd
    spouses,
And ramble abitching thro' all the twelve
    houses;
For all your fine features I'll e'en give you
    over,
The charms of a Whore are but plagues to a
    lover.
Get you gone and be pox'd, to your old bully
    Mars,
Let a God be a slave to your Goddesship's
    A——s;
Whilst I'm contempt of your infamous rump,
On my anvil will knock, with a thump, a
    thump-thump!''

The second day after Frank had read these curious old bits to his parents and sister, they were all
delighted by the arrival of young Harry Mortimer
to spend a day with his old school-mate.

To judge by appearances Mr. Etheridge had every cause for the curious desires he had confessed to, two days before. Harry was a really handsome youth of seventeen, with golden coloured hair, the bloom of the peach on his cheeks, and a most love-able pair of deep blue eyes which seemed full of the humid fire of love. He had also a finely developed form, which his close-fitting garments set off to the best advantage, and, above all, what had the most charm for the eyes of his friends as they so heartily welcomed him to their house was the evident precocity of his organs of love, which in their quiescent state showed a most prominent lump in his trousers.

Mrs. Etheridge: "Why Harry, what a fine fellow you have grown since I saw you a year ago. No doubt you are too bashful to kiss Ethel now, but you will surely embrace an old friend like me, who used to nurse you in my arms as a baby," giving him such an amorous hug and smack upon his cheeks that the young fellow blushed up to his eyes.

After luncheon Frank took Harry for a walk, and asking him if he would like to look at their horses, they bent their steps to the stables where the groom Thomas, a fine handsome young fellow of about twenty, was polishing the coats of his charges, at the same time as he emitted that curious hissing which all stablemen so mysteriously accustom themselves to when busy over their work. He did not see the two young gentlemen till they had been watching his operations for a few seconds, but as soon as he did so, respectfully touched his cap and asked them to look at his horses.

Walking into the stable, Thomas, cap in hand, respectfully pointed out all the perfections of his pets and the neatness of all the appointments. Then he conducted them into the harness room, which was at the top of a short flight of stairs.

Thomas was about to close an interior door, which half open gave a view into his own private quarters, when, a sudden idea striking him, Frank said, "You won't mind, Thomas, if we take a peep into your sanctum—unless you have got a young lady you would rather we did not see. I only want to let Mr. Mortimer see how cosy your room is, besides, you know, I have often had a sly smoke with you there on wet days when I was home for the holidays before, and I know you have always got some nice clean glasses in your cupboard, if not anything better than water to offer us. But I have taken care of that and brought a good flask of finest brandy. I got the housekeeper to give me some of papa's real *vieux cognac*. It's ever so old and goes down like milk. Just the thing, Thomas, to keep you up to your work when you have a nice girl. But I forget you never do anything of the sort, eh! How about little Lucy, the under-house-maid, who I hear had to go home with a big belly not long ago?"

"Lord, sir!" said Thomas, quite enjoying Frank's joke, "that'll be another of old Stroker's kids when it's born. He did it when she went up to be taught her confirmation lesson. I'm told he confirmed seven girls in fucking, this examination.

He's a regular ram of a parson, and will soon be the father of all the young'uns in the parish. I wonder Master let Miss Ethel go to him at all. I always suspected the old fellow after the way he treated me."

They entered the snug little bedroom, where everything was a clean as a new pin, and seated themselves on the only two chairs that were there, whilst the groom brought out the glasses and fetched a jug of bright sweet spring water from the pump outside.

Frank, mixing a rather stiffish drop, said, "Now, Thomas, drink the Rev. Mr. Stroker's health, and then tell us all about his tricks with you."

Himself and Harry also took a little of the brandy. And Thomas, pressed to begin, cleared his throat and commenced:

"Well, Mr. Frank and Mr. Mortimer, I don't mind letting you into the secret, but the fact is every time I think of the old rascal's indecency it makes my cock stand, but you must not tell a soul what I now tell you."

"All right, go on, old fellow, just a drop more brandy to encourage your bashfulness, eh!" laughed Frank.

Thomas, wiping his mouth after a good swig at the brandy and water: "Well, sirs, that righteous old sinner, as an Irishman would say, began by asking me questions about who made me. If I knew there was a God and a Devil. Then about the world and the flesh, and so on, a lot of rubbish out of the church prayerbook. 'You know, Thomas, my boy,' he said, 'that the "flesh" means having to do with girls and other dirty indecent things which come into the heads of rude boys. Now tell me if you ever did anything of that kind with other boys or girls?'

"This was rather a poser for me. I didn't like to tell a downright lie and knew I had been a party to one or two little games of that sort, such as we used to do in the hayfield, throwing the girls down, turning up their clothes, and showing them our cocks, which no doubt the old rascal knew. I could feel my face was turning quite red with confusion. 'Ha, I see what it is, Thomas! I must thoroughly examine you and tell by the look of your penis' (that is the word I think he used, but you know he meant my cock), as he ordered me to unbutton and show him my privates, and he would soon tell if I had been up to any of the Devil's wickedness.

"As soon as I was exposed to him he told me to draw the skin of my cock back, which I did.

" 'Do it again, my boy, there now, again—two or three times mind.'

"Then I expect he saw slight signs of a rise, saying, 'Do it quicker—quicker, boy' till I had the horn quite stiff.

" 'My gracious! You're finely grown for your age, Thomas. Now did you never show that to a gal?'

" 'Well, sir,' I said, rather shamefaced at what he was making me do, 'I did once, but only once, sir, and Polly Jones felt it with her hand, and let me feel what her cock was like, too.'

" 'Fine goings on in my parish, 'pon my word,

Thomas, but what sort a thing had she got? Because you know gals have nothing like this,' he said, taking hold of my standing prick.

" 'She'd—she'd only a little crack, sir,' I replied. 'Pray let me go now, sir, I don't like it.' He was regularly frigging me.

" 'Silly boy, here's a half-crown to keep quiet. if you let me handle it a bit, and you shall have another every time you come to me,' he said, giving me the money, and soon frigged me to a spend and then let me go. I didn't think much harm in it, and was very glad to get the parson's half-crowns, so went twice a week for examination. He wasn't satisfied with just frigging me, but sometimes went down on his knees and sucked my cock till I spent in his mouth, which I liked better, but when he wanted me to do the same for him, and even offered me a sovereign, I wouldn't do it, only let him rub his great cock against my belly and balls, and then he would spend, holding the head of my prick against his own and so drawing his own foreskin over it. Then I had the sovereign never to open my lips about it, and at last was confirmed."

Frank now gave Thomas a drop more brandy and asked him if he would like to be mesmerized, adding, "If you are game to let me, you will then have to answer truthfully any questions I ask and do everything I tell you."

Thomas: "Now, Mr. Frank, you are trying to get at me—as if I would believe that. I ain't afraid. You may try."

Frank: "Then look me steadily in the face, and let me hold you by your two thumbs."

Thomas: "All right, sir, but I be sure you can't make me do as you say."

For a little while he resisted the effects of Frank's mesmeric art, but in less than five minutes his eyes had a quite vacant look, and in obedience to his young master he seated himself on the side of the bed.

"Now, Harry, let me do you as well, as I have an idea I want to carry out."

"You may take hold of my thumbs as you did with Thomas, but I defy you to mesmerize me," said Harry, laughing.

"That's too bad," replied Frank with a smile, "but there's no harm in trying what I can do, old fellow, eh?"

It was a hard task to fix the gaze of his youthful companion, but by patience and perseverance Frank succeeded at last in putting him also into a perfect state of mesmeric sleep.

"Now, my fine fellows, I shall be well rewarded for my trouble before I bring you round again, and it's my turn before I fetch Papa on the scene, I think."

He stripped himself, and ordered his two subjects to do the same, put a small box of cold cream under the pillow of the bed so as to be at hand, then contemplated and handled the young groom and his friend.

Thomas was furnished with a lovely tosser, which swelled rapidly under his touches as he uncovered the ruby head and gently pulled the foreskin backward and forward.

"Now, Thomas, keep yourself stiff by gentle

frigging, but mind not to spend till I order you,"
he said; then he turned to the beautiful Harry
Mortimer, who came to his side as soon as ordered.
He was indeed an Adonis—splendidly shaped in
every limb, delightfully plump and firm white
flesh, rosy cheeks, sparkling blue eyes—but Frank
was so engrossed with his jewel of a prick, which
was a perfect gem of the first water, nearly eight
inches long when erect, as white and hard as ivory,
yet of velvety softness to the touch, and set in a
bed of soft, curly, golden-brown hair, which or-
namented the roots and shaded the full bag of
tricks in their receptacle below.

How Frank handled, caressed, and kissed this
treasure of love, as he ejaculated, "Oh, Papa, oh
Mamma, what a thrill the sight of this will give
you both. But I must enjoy it first!"

Placing himself on the bed, sitting up with his
back supported by a pillow, he ordered Thomas to
straddle his lap. Taking up the box of cream, he
first anointed the head of his own impatient priapus, then did the same to Thomas' fundament,
working his two fingers well in it, which made the
groom's prick throb and stiffen enormously. Then
Frank adjusted his tool to the wrinkled orifice; in
obedience to his mysterious influence Thomas
slowly impaled himself upon it, till his buttocks
embraced its whole length and Frank had his man's
cock deliciously chafing and rubbing between their
naked bellies at every movement. Passing his hands
under Thomas' armpits, Harry was made to come
forwards behind the groom and present his
glorious prick over the left shoulder so that Frank

TWO NOVELS

could take that lovely ruby head in his mouth, whilst his hands drew back the foreskin and tickled and played with its appendages, the mere touch of which filled Frank with maddening lust.

Never had he experienced such extasy and erotic fury as this conjunction with his groom and friend now caused him to feel, he thrilled from head to toe with voluptuous excitement as his spendings seemed to shoot from him again and again, with a very few seconds between each emission, whilst Harry on his part deluged his mouth and lips with the balmy juice of his virginity and Thomas also flooded his belly with convulsive jets of spunk, all of them being so young and vigorous they seemed almost inexhaustible.

At last Frank began to feel it was too much and sank back, overcome by such an acme of enjoyment, as his prick dropped gradually out of the groom's fundus.

Presently recovering himself a little, he took a sip of neat brandy, hastily dressed himself, and willing his subjects to lie quietly on the bed till he came back, he ran with bated breath, and flushed as he was with delight, to call his father and mother to the scene.

They all came back together after the lapse of a few minutes. Papa and Mamma, on entering the little bedroom over the stable, were struck at once by the entrancing sight which met their eyes, of these two beautiful young fellows lying naked on the bed; but in a minute or two both of them threw off all their clothing, in order to thoroughly avail themselves of the treat provided by their dutiful son.

Frank, by his influence, now willed Harry to kneel up on the bed on his hands and knees, whilst Thomas was to lie flat on his back.

Mr. Etheridge, who had brought a fine dildo with him, now put cold cream on it and also on Harry's bum-hole, then inserting the instrument slowly it gradually won its way in, and he watched its effects with delight as young Mortimer's cock began to stand again in all its previous glory. He mounted on the couch behind him, and withdrawing the dildo, put his own rampant prick in its place, having first lubricated it with cold cream, then clasping his arms around the dear youth, he frigged that fine prick, exactly as Frank had seen the professor do with the boy at college.

Mrs. Etheridge waited a few moments watching her spouse's operation till her blood was so fired with amorous excitement that she at once seized upon Thomas' cock, which was lying rather limp between his fine thighs, then forcing his legs a little further apart, she gamahuched him and licked his splendid balls till he was as stiff as ever; then mounting upon her man she slowly impaled herself upon his luscious battering ram as she lowered her body till her lips met his in a fiery voluptuousness, to which, under Frank's mysterious influence, the groom responded with all the ardour of his nature.

For a few moments Mrs. Etheridge continued to kiss and thrust her tongue into Thomas' mouth, whilst she kept her buttocks steady and revelled in the sense of possession which that fine prick afforded her, as her cunt felt throughly gorged by the delicious morsel.

Frank, who had intended to enjoy the scene as as passive spectator, was again fired by the sight of such a voluptuous group, his prick beginning to stiffen again, notwithstanding his previous exhaustion, so mounting on the bed he faced his Papa, and letting down his trousers presented his half erect cock to Harry Mortimer's lips, as he willed him to take it in his mouth and suck it lusciously. The youth's lips opened mechanically, the very first touch of them sending a thrill of pleasure through Frank's frame so that he stiffened up immediately, and fucked the boy's mouth gently, so as not to come again too soon.

Mr. and Mrs. Etheridge both spent quickly, being each of them so excited by the idea of what they were doing, but keeping their places they all went on without stopping, Papa frigging his dear boy Harry, and making his prick spend copiously, receiving the love juice in his hand and rubbing it deliciously over the balls and shaft of the cock he was caressing.

They kept it up deliberately and slowly for some time, so as to enjoy the two fine young fellows to the utmost, then all come together with screams and cries of extasy—Frank seeming to control the whole party by his mesmeric influence in such a way that their very souls vibrated in accordance with his wishes, the enjoyment of father, mother, and son being simply inexpressible.

"Ah, Frank, my dear boy," sighed Mr. Etheridge, "you have afforded us a heavenly treat, but it must now come to an end or we may some of us actually expire under such excessive emotions."

After dressing and willing the two subjects also to assume their clothes, Papa and Mamma went away. Frank recalled Thomas and Harry to consciousness and bantered them about the games he had made them go through at his command. "Would you believe it? You did anything I ordered —sucking each other's pricks, and frigging each other, and doing exactly what I liked to order."

Neither of them would believe it, saying they had only been off for a very short time and that he had tumbled the bed to make believe what he said of them was true. At the same time both admitted having had very confused though pleasing dreams.

A few days after what has just been related, Harry Mortimer paid them another visit, which the family council had resolved should be a regular "mesmeric séance."

Besides their young friend they had invited the rector of the parish, Dr. Stroker, and his two nieces, Blanche and Ada Manners, very pretty brunettes of sixteen and fifteen.

The day passed delightfully on the grounds where they played croquet, or retired to the summer house for refreshment.

During the course of the afternoon Mamma and the parson took a walk by themselves. Mrs. Etheridge, with assumed unconsciousness, pointing out the beauties of the flowers, or calling his attention to the occasional glimpses of the sea, which they obtained through openings of the landscape, till they neared a rustic seat, where she declared she was so very fatigued she must rest awhile if the Doctor did not object.

Seating herself with a slight sigh of relief, she remarked, "How tiring the game of croquet always seemed," adding, "do you not think it is quite absurd for us old people to join with the young ones in such games?"

"My dear Madame," replied the Doctor, "we are always children as long as we live. We enjoy the games of youth with zest, even if we have not the same powers, and it is the same with love, which so enthralls us that I verily believe the older we get the more enthusiastic we become in its pursuit. Now confess, my dear Mrs. Etheridge, is it not so with you?"

"Fie, Doctor, pray don't take advantage of our secluded position to press that hopeless, wicked suit of yours. Besides, sir," she added with a laugh, "this is, you know, Saturday afternoon, and such thoughts can only be prompted by the devil to drive out of your mind all your ideas for tomorrow's sermon."

The parson now ventured to put his arm round that voluptuous waist, as he drew closer still to his lovely companion, saying, "No fear of that, my dear Madame. Can you guess what my text is to be to-morrow?"

"How could I, you silly man?" said Mrs. Etheridge with a very encouraging smile. "Is it anything out of the common?"

"Well, hem—I think it so, Madame, and one

that will bring your sins of omission to your conscience," answered he.

"Don't keep me in suspense, but tell me at once, you foolish fellow, you know I can't guess."

"Can't guess—can't guess even! How you do dissimulate, Mrs. Etheridge, when I know you're always thinking of it, my dear lady. Well then, it's—it's prick—no, I mean the first commandment—you know what that is surely, look at this fine specimen of the Creator's work, and say if you can despise his command, 'to be fruitful and multiply, and replenish the earth,'" he said, placing in her hand his great big standing priapus which he had let out of his trousers.

The touch was electric, a shiver of desire ran through her whole frame, as her fingers seemed to grasp the lovely jewel without knowing what she was about; her eyes closed and she sank back apparently shocked and helpless on the seat.

"Dear lady," the Doctor went on, "the Devil can never prevent me preaching from that text. I could speak extempore upon it for hours, it was the very first command both to Adam and also to Noah when he came out of the ark. Dear Mrs. Etheridge, let me touch that divine cunt of yours. I can't make out what your husband has been about since the charming Ethel was born that you have had no more children, you surely have not obeyed that commandment!"

His hands were already under her dress, feeling those spendid thighs, and gradually working their way up to the seat of bliss.

Mrs. Etheridge's whole form heaved with emotion, he could feel her quiver under his touches, and mistook it for the modesty of her nature rebelling at the libidinous thoughts which his rude proceeding aroused within her, whereas, in reality, it arose from the unbounded lubricity of her nature, now fired by the intensity of her desires.

The Reverend Dr. Stroker was no timid gallant; he proceeded with rapidity from one liberty to another, throwing the lady into still greater confusion. Pressing his lips to hers, he seemed ready to devour her with his fiery kisses, while Mrs. Etheridge also was utterly bereft of power to resist his advances, so pulling up her clothes he forced his legs between her yielding thighs, and soon brought the nose of Mr. Peaslin to the mark. As it just touched the lips of that seraphic cunt the effect was irresistible on the slightly struggling lady, who suddenly opened her legs as widely as possible to meet his charge, and throwing her arms around his neck, returned his kisses with equal ardour as she sighed, "Oh, I am undone, give it me now, dear Doctor, but oh! oh!! oh!!! how shall we take the Holy Communion to-morrow?" as he thrust so vigorously that she was almost beside herself with delight.

"This is the real communion, to-morrow's ceremony is only a farce. Do you think that anyone is ever really fit according to the rubric? Away with such silly nonsense, there is nothing in heaven or earth to compare with the delights of coition!" And his movements went on, each stroke of that fine cock filling her vagina to repletion, and arousing every muscle and membrane of her body to the acme of felicity.

At last both spent together, and they were lying in the state of lethargic enjoyment when the sound of laughter at a distance soon aroused them to a sense of their exposed position, and they had barely time to set things straight before Mr. Etheridge. Frank, Harry, and the three girls came upon the scene.

No particular remarks were made at the time, but significant glances from Mrs. Etheridge informed her husband and children of the pleasure she had just tasted.

They returned to the house for dinner, and afterwards having adjourned to the drawing room, Mrs. Etheridge ordered the servants to have coffee and refreshments ready in the ante-room, but upon no account to disturb their party, as the Doctor was going to give a scientific lecture.

As soon as the servants were gone the parson expressed his surprise at Mrs. Etheridge's announcement, being, as he said, utterly unprepared to give lectures at a minute's warning. To which the hostess replied with a slightly ironical tone in her voice, "But, Doctor, you told me this afternoon you could lecture upon and illustrate the first commandment at any time. However, if you do not feel equal to lecturing for our amusement, my Frank shall show some of his mesmeric tricks which he acquired in Germany, and you shall be his first subject."

"Not the slightest objection in the world to that,

if it will amuse you, my dear Mrs. Etheridge," replied the rector, "but don't tell me afterwards that I have been confessing to all sorts of scandalous things, because I know these mesmeric lecturers can make their subjects say anything."

During this dialogue Frank had, unobserved by the others, quietly put Miss Blanche into a state of unconsciousness, then turning to Harry told him that if he would submit to be again operated upon, he could make him and the Doctor's niece dance and sing to his orders to amuse the company.

Harry Mortimer was too good-natured to refuse, and after him Frank also put the parson and Ada Manners into the same state, then as he looked around upon his parents and sisters he asked them, with a look of triumph, what the programme was to be.

Ethel: "You left me out of the little party over the stable the other afternoon, so now it is my turn to be considered."

Papa: "By all means, my darling, only say what you wish for."

Ethel: "Then we will all strip, and as I wish particularly to feel that great and reverend prick, I will kneel on the couch and have the Doctor dog fashion, so we can see all what is going on. First make the two girls frig each other, then they shall be made to do the same to Harry and Frank, who will afterwards take their virginities, whilst you and Mamma will be delighted to gamahuche and help the operation, and after that we will be guided by our fancies."

This pleased everyone. The subjects were made

to strip off everything except the ladies' boots and stockings, presenting a most luscious sight to the free-loving family. Then to make up a tableau Frank willed that the Doctor, naked as he was, should take and seat his two nieces on his knees, and under his influence each of the two sisters at once extended a hand to grasp his glorious prick, which at the same time rose in all its pride of strength, so that their delicate hands, one above the other on its shaft, still left the purple head towering above the uppermost by two or three inches at least.

Harry also took his place by the side of Ada, who caressed his stiffened cock with her disengaged hand, whilst Blanche did the same to Frank, who had stripped and stood by her side to complete the group.

Beautiful as was this scene, Ethel lost very little time before she placed herself on the couch on all fours, and as Frank ordered his subjects, the two nieces fairly dragged their uncle by his prick, till they got him up behind Ethel, and planted the head of his fiery steed just within the lips of her longing cunt.

Mr. and Mrs. Etheridge now produced their birch rods, and began to stimulate the parson with a shower of stinging cuts, the tips of the birch often also touching up Ethel's bum or thighs and adding very materially to her erotic enjoyment, as the Doctor fucked in a perfect fury of lust under the effects of the birching, which fairly scored his firm, hard flesh, breaking the skin and drawing little drops of blood.

Meanwhile Frank had conducted Harry Mortimer and the rector's nieces to another part of the
room, and willed the two girls to frig each other.
They were perfectly amenable to his every wish,
Blanche stretching herself at full length on a fine
rug made of the skin of wild cats (which are said
to have such exciting effects on those who recline
upon them).

Ada was made to reverse herself upon her elder
sister, and each opening their legs with the utmost
freedom, frigged and gamahuched each other's cunts
in such a luscious manner as left little doubt in
Frank's mind that the two young girls had often
before had rehearsals of the same game in private.

The mesmerizer and his young friend knelt down
also on the rug on either side of the tribades, and
facing each other, embraced with the most apparent ardour across the bodies of the writhing and
excitable girls. Each of them put an arm round
the other's neck, their lips meeting in the most wanton manner possible as they sucked each other's
tongues, whilst their disengaged hands were applied to their respective pricks, till the spending
moment came upon the group simultaneously—
the two girls almost fainting from excess of pleasure as they emitted their virgin love juice, whilst
the young fellows above them also spent as they
held the noses of their pricks together, letting the
overflow of sperm sprinkle all over Blanche and
Ada below.

The other group had had an equally extatic
finish, Ethel pushing back her bottom upon the
parson's prick at the critical moment with all the

energy of her maddening lust, and receiving within
the inmost recess of her insatiable womb a perfect
torrent of bliss, making her fairly scream with delight as she sank down on the couch from the
voluptuous exhaustion of the moment, the folds of
her cunt tightening and throbbing upon his delighted prick in such a way that it retained its
stiffness, and soon recommenced another thrilling
course with Ethel lying flat under him face downwards. It was a delicious situation—she held him
so tightly, although his prick did not go so far in,
that he screamed out, "Holy Moses, what a fuck!
Her cunt's as tight as a boy's arsehole!" as he clung
to her and ground his teeth in the height of his
excitement.

Mr. Etheridge was behind him now, and using
some cold cream on the Doctor's rough-looking,
brown, wrinkled bottom-hole, presented his cock
to the mark, and clinging tightly round his waist
soon gained admission by the reverend back door.
How tight and warm it was to his excited priapus,
which answered by a thrust to every heave of the
parson's bottom as he fucked the dear girl beneath
him.

Mamma also, not to be left out of the game,
mounted on the long couch, and lying on her back
in front of her daughter, opened her thighs so as to
embrace Ethel's face and present her longing cunt
for her to suck. Then reclining her head and
shoulders on a large cushion, she called for Frank
and Harry to leave the two girls, and come on
either side of her so that they could both present
the heads of their pricks to her lips, whilst she

handled their balls and frigged them till they shot into her mouth a double flow of the nectar of love which she so loved to drain to the very last drop.

Papa revelled in his rear attack as his hand fondled with delight the Doctor's prick and balls at every withdrawal from Ethel's cunt, the lips of which he could also feel as they tenaciously clung round the shaft of that fine instrument, which was giving such pleasure at every thrust.

At this juncture Frank willed the parson to awake from the mesmeric trance. His eyes resumed their wanton intelligence, and as he at once realised the situation, his usual sanctified demeanour caused him to give vent to an assumed exclamation of horror, "How awful, what have they been doing to me!" Then, "Oh, it must be a dream of my old college days, by Jove, how we fucked and buggered at Oxford!"

"That's right, Doctor," laughed Frank, "now you are beginning to fairly comprehend how we are punishing you for taking advantage of Mamma this afternoon, only it's pleasure instead of pain, old boy. But we thought anyone with such a glorious prick as yours ought not to be too hardly treated."

The spasm of pleasure prevented further speech at the moment, fairly carrying away the whole group by the intensity of the sensations which such erratic voluptuousness could not fail to produce upon natures which, after all, were only sustained by the ordinary powers of humanity, in fact it was too exhaustive to allow of further indulgence in venery upon the present occasion. But after recovering a little, the Doctor, who now thoroughly relished the idea, proposed that Harry, Blanche, and Ada should be still kept in their entranced state to afford them amusement, as he said it would be a fine treat to make them tell all the little games they had been up to.

The three subjects were not allowed to dress, but all the others now resumed their clothes, then the parson proceeded to catechise them.

Q.—Blanche, did you ever hear how babies are made?

A.—A girl at school told me the men shove their cocks into the girls, and shoot their spunk into them, which makes the babies.

Q.—Do the girls like to have that done to them?

A.—Yes, it's awfully funny and nice, makes our cunts what they call spend with pleasure.

Q.—Have you ever felt anything of it yourself? Do the girls play at fathers and mothers at school?

A.—Nearly every night we used to change bedfellows for the purpose of having a fresh bit of cock, as we used to call their fingers.

Q.—Go on, tell us all about it.

A.—Some of the girls used a candle or the finger of a glove stuffed out to make a little prick, a well greased carrot was fine I can tell you. Once they nearly drove me mad with delight by fucking me with a carrot, whilst another girl used a tallow candle in my bumhole till nothing but the wick was left. But I felt awfully bad next day, and you can fancy I passed tallow when I went to the closet.

Q.—Well, and how did Ada get on?

A.—She did not sleep in our room, she was with the French governess.

Q.—Now, Ada, you must also tell us all you know.

A.—The French governess was so hairy and rude, she began by tickling my fanny till I didn't know what I was doing, then she laid me back on the bed, and forced her face between my thighs, and sucked my cunny.

Q.—Well, go on, out with everything.

A.—After a while she would lay over me, and make me kiss her great hairy slit. Oh, you should have seen what a lot of hair she had on her belly, as black as jet right up to her navel. And then she used to wriggle about, and wet all my lips and face, which she called spending. A favorite game of hers was to make me frig her by forcing as much as I could of one of my titties into her cunt, which seemed to drive her almost wild; she would kiss my legs, feet, and any part she could reach in a frantic way whilst I was doing it.

Q.—Did she never do the same thing to you?

A.—Yes, it was awfully fine to feel her titty and nipple rubbing just inside the lips of my little cunny, I believe she made me spend—at least, I fainted and found myself all wet afterwards.

Q.—What other rude games have you been up to, by yourself or with your sister?

A.—When we were home for the holidays we used to frig each other with our fingers or titties, the latter was quite a new idea to Blanche. Then we got a little dog to suck our cunnies. Ah, that was another fine game, his tongue seemed to go everywhere, and drive us wild with delight. One day we took it in turns to suck his little prick whilst he was licking one of us—it was beautiful, but drove the little beast almost mad. At last we had to tie a stone round his neck and drown the poor thing, because he was always getting under our clothes.

Q.—Now, Harry, when did you first touch a girl's thing?

A.—I suppose I was about twelve when that happened. My aunt Clara, a very beautiful young widow of twenty-three, who had just lost my uncle (her husband) in the terrible Clayton Tunnel accident, and I may here add that what hurt her sensitive feelings almost more than his loss was the fact that the gay young fellow had taken a girl on the sly with him to Brighton for the day, and you know it was on the return journey that the collision occurred. Well, her grief and thoughts of his conduct, she said, made her so nervous and low spirited that she begged my Mamma to allow little Harry, as she called me, to go and stay with her for a time as companion. Every morning she would come into my bedroom to awaken me with a loving kiss, pulling off the bed-clothes, and playing me all sorts of tricks to make me get up. On one occasion, feeling unusually tired, I begged she would let me lay only a few minutes longer, as I drew her beautiful face down to my lips and smothered her with kisses. I was almost uncovered at the moment, it was a bright May morning, and the glorious sun was flooding the apartment with his beams of light and warmth. "My darling boy," she said softly, "I have a slight headache, and will rest on the bed by your side a little while," throwing her arms around me, and nestling her soft cheeks against mine. I soon felt her hands wandering over every part of my body, but it was so nice that when I felt her touch my naked thigh, I felt a curious kind of alloverishness, and my little prick stood as stiff as a poker. At last she touched even that. My eyes were apparently closed, pretending to be in a doze, but I could see the blush that came into her cheeks, and felt her give a kind of shudder all over. She caressed my little cocky for a moment or two, which gave me a kind of longing for her to go on. I could see she was greatly agitated, but my own sense of pleasure prevented me thinking much about that. My heart seemed to go out to her in a gush of love, as I suddenly opened my eyes, and throwing my arms around her neck once more, kissed her again and again.

How her eyes sparkled, and she seemed to blush deeper than ever, but her soft hand never let go of the little treasure she had secured.

"Harry, my dear boy, is your little affair often like this? It is quite unnaturally hard," she asked me in a low, husky kind of whisper. "Perhaps you are ill, my dear, let me see," saying which she threw back the bed-clothes, and examined my privates, handling my stiff pintle very tenderly, as if she really thought there might be something the matter with me, and finished by kissing my cock and taking the poor thing in her mouth as she said it must be quite painful to bear. You may guess that the only effect of her endearments was to make my affair swell up bigger than I had ever known it, as well as putting me in a kind of flutter all over, in fact I can't describe how she made me feel.

The next night I had been asleep about a couple of hours when I was suddenly awakened by someone bringing a light into my room; it was Auntie Clara in her nightdress. "Harry," she said, "I feel so nervous, pray do come and sleep with me, I don't like to ask the servants, and you can slip back into your room in the morning."

I was too pleased to say no, and soon found myself in her bed nestling close to her, with my face between her soft bubbies. She at once asked me if my affair was stiff, and seemed astonished to find it again hard when she caressed it, as I told her it had been quite limp all day.

She kissed me again and again, telling me it proved I was getting to be a man. "But, Harry darling, you must never say a word about it. Would you like to be my little husband and always sleep with me?"

"Oh, Auntie, that would be delightful, would you marry me if I was a man?" I asked in reply.

"Yes, darling, and I will wait till you grow up, if you promise now to be my husband, and keep secret everything between us."

How we played together after I gave her my solemn promise. She let me feel her all over, got out of bed, lighted three or four candles, and stripped herself quite naked for me to see what she was like. She made me kiss her lovely cunt, all covered and shaded by dark chestnut hair as it was, and assured me I should soon also have hair round the roots of my cock, then she showed me how to be a husband to her, and made me work my little cock in her till she almost drowned it in her spendings.

So you see I have been engaged to be married ever since then, and every time we have a chance Aunt Clara accords me all the rights of a husband. She says we have only to wait a year or two now, as she has a handsome income, enough for us both if my parents object.

This was the end of the séance, the subjects were all put in order and restored to consciousness, and the Doctor quietly whispered to Mr. and Mrs. Etheridge that he should like to bring his two nieces after the Sunday evening service, to be mesmerized again and have their maidenheads taken, it would be such a treat to see it done.

It is not necessary to weary the reader by full details of how Frank and Harry did this for them, to complete the satisfaction of their reverend uncle, who again enjoyed the delights of being sandwiched between his host and hostess, and helped them to realise every erotic imagination of their hearts.

By way of conclusion it will perhaps be interesting to relate the experiences of a young lady (none other than Minette) who paid a visit to this charming family in later days.

The account is taken from a letter sent to a gentleman friend, to whom she was much attached at the time.

One day we were all taken into what I imagined to be the drawing room, but afterwards ascertained it was a place strictly confined to the private use of the family and that but one confidential servant was ever allowed to enter it, for the purpose of cleaning, dusting, and keeping it in order. The walls were hung with pictures of the most exciting character, and in the centre of the room was a huge bed, covered with crimson velvet and stuffed with down, but without any of the ordinary bed-clothing, instead there were a quantity of cushions variously shaped and also covered with velvet. Some of these were fitted with concealed dildoes, so that when pressed between the thighs the most delightful frigging could be produced. Some were fitted with artificial cunts for the use of gentlemen, if they felt so inclined. There were flogging machines of every description, and various articles of furniture for supporting the body in peculiar positions which might be required while being fucked, sucked, or buggered.

The door was no sooner closed than I was seized by Frank and his mother and tumbled on the bed, where they rummaged every part of my body, bottom-hole, cunt, and bubbies, and at last forced one of the dildo-cushions between my thighs and compelled me to frig myself upon it, while they pulled up my clothes and slapped my poor arse for some minutes without mercy, laughing and enjoying my screams as my tender rump plunged up and down in exquisite pain.

Ethel was helping them by sitting on my shoulders so that I was quite powerless, but when they presently desisted from that cruel slapping and I felt tongue, finger, or prick alternately forced up my bottom, it was delicious—the heat of the previous infliction making me feel so lecherous that the spunk actually spurted from my quim as I wriggled myself up and down on the dildo.

Ethel I found also (as soon as the paroxysm of spending had allayed my feelings a little, and I was allowed to look around) was sucking her father's prick, whilst he was frigging her.

Next, the servant Maud entered the room and was immediately stripped to the skin and bound to a flogging machine, where they birched her deliciously (at least it looked so to me, although she screamed and writhed about in pain, and begged for mercy as the tears streamed down her face), till she was on the verge of spending. She was then left to suffer the agonies of unsatisfied desire, while we enacted all the most lascivious things we could think of in her sight.

I took Mr. Etheridge's prick and frigged it between my bubbies, whilst he sucked the prick of his son.

We then tickled the girl's inflamed cunt with stinging nettles, which increased her excitement till she seemed mad with erotic delirium, and Mr. Etheridge, to my horror, proposed that we should injure her as a finish to our orgy for that evening.

Mr. Etheridge drove his tremendously inflamed prick into her bottom-hole, the position in which she was suspended making the operation awfully painful. Frank fucked the poor girl in the cunt. Mrs. Etheridge and Ethel, with savage pleasure, each sucked and bit the victim's nipples, causing her to writhe and scream in agony. The two fuckers were at the same time frigging mother and daughter, whilst they passed the sensation on to me by also manipulating my cunt and bottom.

Suddenly I heard a yell of agony, and found that Frank, just in the moment of spending, had stabbed the girl with a small dagger which he had concealed in his hand.

We all spent together with mingled cries of lust and delight, the convulsive movements of the suffering girl adding immensely to the intensity of this voluptuous emission.

However, our victim was not seriously hurt. She was convalescent in a week's time, but was ultimately murdered, while in the act of spending, by a voluptuary with whom she afterwards lived.

Before my visit terminated there was another orgy, in which Harry Mortimer introduced his Aunt Clara to this amiable family circle. Mesmerism was now quite unnecessary,

Harry being as willing a votary to the worship of Priapus as could possibly be desired
by his erotic friends.

The principal scene of the evening was a
group in which the beautiful Aunt Clara rode
a St. George upon Mr. Etheridge, had Harry
in her bottom-hole, Frank's prick in her
mouth, her two hands frigging Mrs. Etheridge and Ethel as they stood by the side of
the couch, whilst your *chère amie*, not to be
left out of the game, was behind Harry, my
left hand passed round his loins, caressing his
fine prick and balls as it worked in and out
of her beautiful brown bumhole, whilst my
right forefinger postilioned him behind.

You must imagine the excitement of this
group so voluptuously arranged; it requires
to be engaged in such a scene to fully appre-
ciate all its heavenly delights—description is
simply impossible!

FINIS

LAURA
MIDDLETON

HER BROTHER
and
HER LOVER

The remarks which Emily had made regarding the share Laura Middleton had had in opening up her ideas on the subject of the mysteries in which she had now been fully initiated had not escaped my observation. It so happened that at that very time I was under an engagement to pay a visit to the Middletons, who were very distant relations of my mother. It of course occurred to me that it was possible I might be able to turn the information I had thus acquired to some account. Laura and I were old friends. She was about two years older than I, a very handsome, fine-looking girl but, as I had then fancied, upon rather a larger scale than quite suited my taste. We had always been on very good terms as children, but she had a sort of haughty, imperious air which, joined to the difference in our ages, had operated in a manner that would have prevented me from thinking of taking any liberties with her; and she was about the last person in the world I should have been disposed to imagine addicted to the amusements in which Emily had participated with her.

When I again met her on arriving at their country seat, I found that a considerable change had taken place in her person, but probably this was merely the natural result that the preceding two years, during which I had not seen her, had worked upon a girl at her time of life, by fully developing the proportions and fining down the parts of the figure which at an earlier period might have appeared too prominent. I too had grown considerably during this period, more so in proportion than she had, and now her height by no means appeared to me to be too great; and, altogether, I could not help acknowledging to myself that I had rarely seen a handsomer or finer-looking woman. She still retained somewhat of her haughty air, though softened down, and I could hardly fancy, when looking at her, that Emily's account of her behaviour in the hours when she gave herself up to enjoyment could be true. I soon, however, became aware of circumstances that tended to corroborate the tale, and which put me in the way of making advances to her, which I hastened to do.

LAURA MIDDLETON

When it came to be time to dress for dinner, Lady Middleton said to me that she had presumed on our relationship to put me into the family wing of the house, as the arrival of some unexpected visitors had made her change the destination of the room she had previously intended for me. She said she had no doubt I would find the one set apart for me quite comfortable, for the only objection to it, and which prevented her from being able to put a stranger into it, was that it opened into another room which would have to be occupied by her son Frank, who was expected home from school in a short time. This last room, in consequence of some alterations made in building an addition to the house, had no separate entrance, but opened into the two rooms on each side, and as the one on the other side was occupied by his sister and aunt, Frank would have to enter through mine. She said I must keep him in order and make him behave himself, and if I had any trouble with him to let her know. I had not seen my young namesake for about two years, but I recollected him as a fine, high-spirited, very handsome boy about twelve or thirteen years of age, always getting into some scrape or other and always getting out of them somehow in such a fearless, good-humoured manner that it was impossible for anyone to be angry with him. So I said I should be delighted to renew my acquaintance with my young friend, and that I had not the least doubt but that we should get on very pleasantly.

On going to my room to dress for dinner, I found a servant-girl engaged in making some of the arrangements which the change of apartments had necessitated. On my entrance she was going to leave the room, but seeing that she was a very nice-looking young girl, I said she need not run away in such a hurry, that surely she was not afraid of me. She gave me an arch look as if taking the measure of my capacities, and replied with a smile that she did not think she need be afraid of such a nice-looking young gentleman. This I thought was a fair challenge, and it induced me to take a better look at her. I found she was a very well made country girl of about nineteen, with some very promising points about her. I therefore kept her in conversation for a short time, while I went on with my washing operation. Finding she was in no hurry to leave me, I went up to her as she was engaged in putting the bed in order and snatched a few kisses. I then commenced playing with her bubbies and taking some further liberties with her. As my proceedings met with very little resistance, beyond a few exclamations of "Oh for shame, I did not expect such conduct from you," I proceeded with my researches and without much difficulty I succeeded in raising her petticoats and getting possession of her stronghold. On insinuating my finger within it, I found it to be tighter and even more inviting than I had anticipated.

She soon became excited with my caresses and the titillation which my finger kept up without her fortress, and I succeeded in laying her upon the bed and throwing up her clothes so as to disclose it fairly to my view. I found a fine, fresh, white belly and a pair of plump, handsome thighs with a very pretty little opening tolerably well shaded with light brown hair. Altogether it was a very desirable prospect, and I thought that failing anything better I might manage to find a good deal of enjoyment in her charms. Slipping off my trousers, therefore, I jumped up beside her on the bed, and throwing my arms round her, I got upon her and attempted to introduce myself into the fortress. But here I found greater resistance than I had anticipated from her previous conduct.

I had observed, however, the effect my caresses had produced on her senses. I thought the best plan would be to endeavour to excite them still more. So, insinuating the finger of one hand again into the critical spot, and with the other drawing my shirt over my head so as to leave myself entirely naked, I raised myself on my knees beside her, exhibiting my standard fully erected, flaming fiercely before her eyes. While continuing to excite her by the movements of my finger, I said I was sure she would not be cruel enough to refuse me, but would take pity upon the little suppliant that was begging so hard for admittance. Taking hold of her hand I placed it upon the stiff object and made her grasp it as it throbbed and beat with the excitement under which I was labouring. Her eyes were fixed upon the lovely object thus exposed to her gaze, and I could easily see from the flushing of her face and the sparkling of her eyes what a powerful impression I had made upon her.

All she said was, "Oh, but if John should know of it."

I immediately replied, "But why should John

know anything about it? You don't suppose I am such a mean wretch as to tell anybody of what we may do, and if you only keep your own secrets no one need ever know anything about it.

"But perhaps," I continued, "you think this little gentleman," and I shoved the furious member backwards and forwards two or three times in her hand as she still continued to grasp it, "is not so big as John's and won't give you so much pleasure, but only let me try and I shall do all I can to pleasure you."

"Oh no, it is not that," said she hastily, squeezing the little object convulsively in her grasp, and as I bent down to kiss her, she whispered, "I can't resist you any longer, but you must bolt the door, and if anybody comes I can get away through Miss Laura's room. She won't tell anything; I can easily make her keep quiet."

This speech not a little astonished me, for from what I knew of Laura I thought she was the last person in the world to make a confidante of her waiting-maid. But I was aware that this was not the moment to expect any explanation, so I jumped out of bed, bolted the door, and speedily returned to the charge, when I found that the opposing party had given up all idea of defence and was quite ready to meet my advances. Stretching herself out in the most favourable position, she allowed me again to mount upon her and, taking hold of the instrument of love, she herself guided it to the proper quarter.

To my surprise, however, the entrance was much more difficult than I had expected and I soon found that I had overrated Master John's capacities and that the fortress, though not a maiden one, had not previously been entered by so large a besieging force. With some little exertion on my part, aided by every means in her power, though she winced a good deal at the pain I put her to, I at length succeeded in effecting my object and penetrated to a depth which from her exclamation of delight when she found me fairly imbedded within her, and from certain other symptoms, I felt certain had never been reached previously. Once fairly established within my new quarter we mutually exerted our utmost endeavours to gratify each other as well as ourselves, and the result of our efforts soon led, much to the satisfaction of both parties, in the temporary subjugation of both the contending forces. Gratified by finding that the issue had been much more satisfactory than I had expected, and not having had an opportunity for some time previously of indulging myself so agreeably, I, much to her surprise and joy, retained possession of the stronghold with my forces so slightly weakened by their late defeat as to give immediate promise of a renewed attack.

Telling her to be still for a few minutes and that we should shortly enjoy ourselves again, I began to question her regarding the matters in which I felt interested. I thought it better at first not to allude to Laura, so I commenced by inquiring about John, and I soon found that the one subject led to the other. It appeared that John was the under-groom whose duty it was to attend upon Miss Laura when she rode out. John had courted

Betsy for some time previously and had been admitted to all the privileges of a husband on condition that he should marry her as soon as he could obtain a situation which would enable him to support her.

Betsy, it seems, was rather jealous, and John, to teaze her, had pretended that he was on terms of intimacy with his young Mistress, a statement for which there was not the slightest foundation. Betsy's suspicions, however, being once roused, were not easily set at rest, and this led her to pay more attention than previously to her young Mistress's proceedings. She had sometimes wondered what induced Laura to go out by herself almost every morning before breakfast, and now fancying that it might be for the purpose of meeting John, she resolved to watch her and ascertain if her suspicions were correct. She acordingly followed her, and found that she invariably made her way to a small summer house at a little distance from the house. Here John never made his appearance, but curious to know what Laura was about, Betsy continued her spying until she one day ascertained that, instead of amusing herself with John's article, Miss Laura resorted to the place for the purpose of consoling herself with a very insufficient substitute for what Betsy had suspected to be the offending member.

As Laura slept in the same room with her aunt she had no opportunity of thus indulging herself.

I drew all this gradually from her, leading her on by degrees, and trying to make it appear that I had no particular interest in the subject. Her story,

however, had such an effect upon a certain part of
my body, which was still imbedded within her,
that she could not help feeling as she proceeded
with her tale the impression it made upon me. Indeed when she came to relate the discovery she had
made, I was obliged to stop her and proceed to a
repetition of our enjoyment in order to allay the
fire which had been so fiercely lighted up within
me. When I had brought the second engagement to
a still more satisfactory conclusion than the first,
I found it was time for me to get on with my
dressing so as not to be too late for dinner, and
Betsy volunteered her services to assist as valet.
The lewd little monkey, however, was too intent
upon examining the course from which she had
derived so much pleasure to do anything except
fondle and caress it, and seeing the pleasure it
evidently gave her, I allowed her to do as she liked.
While she amused herself with tickling and squeezing the accessories, handling the principal object,
kissing it, inserting it in her mouth and sucking it,
and doing everything in her power to restore it to
the imposing attitude which had pleased her so
much, I endeavoured with as much apparent un-
concern as I could assume to ascertain every particular as to Laura.

Betsy however was too quick not to discover
what I was after, and said to me, "Come, come,
I see quite well how it is with you—you would
like this pretty little gentleman I am playing with
to take the place of its substitute between Miss
Laura's thighs. Oh! you need not try to deceive
me—I felt how it swelled up within me whenever

I mentioned her name, and how firm and stiff it grew when I told you what I had seen. Well, it would be almost a pity not to let you take compassion upon her; it is very hard she should be reduced to such a miserable contrivance when she might have such a delicious charmer as this to amuse herself with. But I am afraid you would have some difficulty in getting it in, more than you had with me, why her little plaything is not much bigger than my finger; even John's, though it is not near so big as this, is better than it. But as for this wicked fellow I can hardly grasp it in my hand, and I don't see how you will ever be able to make it enter into such a little chink as she has. However, I dare say you will be able to manage it somehow. Come, I shall make a bargain with you: if you will take John as your groom, so as to let us be married before my belly gets big, as I am afraid it will do after this naughty fellow has been into it, I shall do all I can to enable you to enjoy Miss Laura, and I have no doubt we shall soon find means to accomplish it. What do you say?"

I replied that I was afraid such an arrangement would hardly answer. In the first place, I could not turn away my present servant, and secondly, I was afraid that if John were in my service he might perhaps be apt to be jealous of his master.

She laughed and said that would never do. She, however, soon came to an agreement that I should exert myself to find a better situation for John, and I promised her that if I succeeded with Laura, she should make her a present of fifty pounds as a wedding gift on condition that she acted in all respects as I desired and exerted herself to promote my object and conceal our proceedings from everyone. She stipulated that she was sometimes to have the enjoyment of the charming article which she still continued to fondle, and this I willingly promised, but I warned her that she must be very careful that her Mistress should not suspect our intercourse in the least, as I was quite sure from what I knew of her proud disposition it would ruin all my hopes, as she would never consent to be the rival of her waiting-maid. I easily satisfied her that even for her own sake the utmost caution was absolutely necessary, and having now obtained all the information she could give me and the dinner bell ringing, I hastened to the drawing room.

If I had perceived an alteration in Laura's appearance, she had evidently been no less struck with the change that had taken place in my person, and she expressed her surprise at my having grown so much. I fancied I could perceive that there was some curiosity to ascertain what was the extent of the change which had taken place in a certain quarter, and I caught her eyes more than once glancing in a direction where she must have perceived symptoms of a growth at least corresponding to that of the other parts of my body. I was induced to think that she was by no means displeased with the discovery from her manner towards me, which instead of being as formerly haughty and condescending was now frank and friendly. On entering the drawing room I found that Sir Hugh had not yet made his appearance, and that it would still be a few minutes before we went to dinner. I was conscious that the fingering which Betsy had kept up during the whole time I was dressing had again raised a flame in me which I had not had time to quench, and I turned into the music room to take advantage of the few minutes to calm myself down, that I might not make an exhibition before the rest of the party. Laura had observed me, and thinking that the movement arose from shyness at meeting a party of comparative strangers, she came to me and entered into conversation. The charms of her person, more especially after all that had just passed with Betsy regarding her, again raised the flame to an even greater height than before, and the effect was plainly visible through a pair of thin trousers. I soon saw by her heightened colour that the consequences were not unobserved by her. I was afraid at first that she might be annoyed by so open a demonstration of the effects of her charms, but to my great delight she showed no symptom of being offended, but continued to converse with me, and, I thought, rather enjoyed the confusion which the rampantness of the offending member at first occasioned me. Finding this to be the case, I soon recovered my self-possession, and being desirous to make as great an impression on her senses as possible, I placed myself so that I could not be observed by any of the party in the drawing room, and instead of attempting to conceal it, I allowed the protuberance in front to become even more prominent, indeed so much so, as to enable her to form a pretty accurate idea of its size and shape. She took no notice of this, but I knew it could not escape her observation. When a general move was made to the dining room, she took my arm and said that, as I was a stranger, I must allow her to take charge of me, until I became a little better acquainted with the company. I willingly assented, and for the rest of the evening I attached myself to her. Without attempting to take any liberties with her, I omitted no opportuniy of letting her see the full effect of her beauty and charms upon my senses.

The next morning I was up early and on the lookout. From Betsy's description I had not been able exactly to understand how I could manage to surprise Laura during her amusement, and I determined to watch and follow her and be guided by circumstances. Sometime before the breakfast hour I saw her leave the house by a side door and proceed through a part of the park which was a good deal shaded with trees. I took advantage of the shelter thus afforded me to trace her steps, unperceived, until I came in sight of the summer house, but to my dismay, I found that it was impossible to follow her any further without being discovered. The building was circular, consisting of woodwork to the height of about four feet and above that glass all round. It was situated in the centre of a flower plot of considerable extent in which the bushes were kept down and not allowed to attain any size.

It was therefore admirably adapted for the purpose to which it had been applied, as no one approaching it could well see what passed within, while the party in the interior could command an uninterrupted view all round and discover any intruder at some distance. I was quite aware that it was most important to avoid giving her any alarm or making her suspect I had any idea of her proceedings, and I resolved not to attempt to approach her that morning. So, selecting a tree which was situated in such a manner as to command a complete view of the summer house, I swung myself up into it and soon gained a position from which, with the assistance of a small telescope I had taken with me, I could obtain a good view of her proceedings. I very soon discovered that Betsy's story was perfectly correct. She had apparently no time to spare, for, taking out the little instrument from its place of concealment, she seated herself on a couch from which she could command a view of the approach from the house. Then, extending her thighs, she drew up her petticoats and, inserting the counterfeit article in the appropriate place, began her career of mock pleasure.

I watched all her proceedings with the greatest enjoyment, and such was the effect produced upon me that I could not help following her example. I drew forth my excited member and, as she thrust the little bijou in and out of the delicious cavity in which I so longed to replace it with a better substitute, I responded to every movement of her hand by an up-and-down friction upon the ivory pillar, with such effect that, when she sunk back upon the couch after having procured for herself as much pleasure as such a makeshift could afford, I felt the corresponding efforts produce a similar effect upon my own excited reality, which, throbbing and beating furiously, sent forth a delicious shower of liquid bliss.

I allowed her to get up and return to the house without her perceiving me, and when we met at breakfast she was not even aware I had been out. The day passed very pleasantly. She was evidently flattered with the devotion I showed her and seemed noways indisposed to try to what length her encouragement might carry me, probably thinking that she could at any time check my advances should they become too forward.

In the course of the day I again visited the summer house and ascertained that I had no chance of surprising her there without making some alteration in it, which it would take a little time to effect, but which I resolved to have made if I found I could not succeed otherwise. In the meantime, I resolved to try the effect of a bold stroke.

Getting up early the next morning I proceeded directly to the summer house and waited there till she made her appearance. Having made certain that she was alone, I stretched myself on the couch as nearly as possible in the attitude she had assumed the previous morning. I then unbuttoned my trousers and drew them down below my knees and at the same time turned up my shirt above my waist thus exhibiting the whole forepart of my person entirely naked. Then grasping my stiffly erected weapon in my hand, I exhibited myself performing the same operation which I had witnessed her engaged in the previous morning. She came in without the least suspicion and, on entering the place, had at once a full view of my nearly naked figure extended at full length on the couch and engaged in performing an operation the nature of which she could not possibly misunderstand.

She seemed struck with astonishment—so much that she remained motionless for more than a minute, during which I watched her with intense curiosity. Her face and neck, so far as visible, flushed till they were almost of a purple hue, and her eyes were fixed upon the stiffly erected column up and down which my hand was gently moving. I was in great hopes that the sight had produced the effect I desired. But no. Suddenly recovering herself, she exclaimed, "For shame, Sir," and turning away hastily left the place before I had time to rise and interrupt her. I would fain have followed her and tried to induce her to return, but I would not allow my passions to carry me so far as to do what might injure her irreparably in the event of anyone being about the grounds and seeing me in the condition in which I then was.

Before I could replace my dress so as to be able to venture out, she had gone so far that she had reached the house ere I could make up to her.

When we met at breakfast she took no notice of what had passed; nor could I discover any difference in her manner to me, beyond her heightened colour when we exchanged the morning greeting as if we had not met before. But she carefully avoided any opportunity of our being left alone, though I could sometimes detect her eyes glancing towards me when she thought she was not observed, and more particularly in the direction of the part of which she had obtained a first glance that morning.

Having gone so far with her, I was determined to try at least whether I could not get a little farther. So in the evening when a dance was got up I asked her to waltz with me in such an open manner that she could not easily make any excuse for not doing so. As soon as I got an opportunity of saying a few words unheard, I whispered to her, "Come, come, Laura, this is too bad of you to be offended at me for doing the very same thing I saw you doing in the same place yesterday morning."

In an instant her face turned perfectly scarlet and then as pale as death, and I am certain she would have fallen to the ground had I not supported her. In a few seconds she recovered herself a little and in a suppressed but earnest tone she whispered, "Hush, hush for God's sake."

I led her out of the room into the conservatory and pressed her to sit down on a bench. She objected to this, saying, "Not here; not here," pointing at the same time to the door at the opposite side leading into a rosary which was not overlooked from the drawing room. I there placed her on a seat and sat down beside her and waited for a few minutes, till her emotion should subside.

Finding that she was still quite overcome and remained silent, trembling, and evidently greatly agitated by the discovery that her secret was known to me, I said to her, "Laura, dearest, you need not be in the least alarmed, your secret is quite safe with me, and nothing shall ever induce me to say a word to anyone regarding it, nor need you fear, my own darling, that I shall take advantage of it to make you do anything you don't like."

She made no reply but at the same time she offered no resistance to the caresses I ventured to bestow upon her, and I even fancied that the warm kiss I imprinted on her lips was faintly returned. I went on to say, "I cannot tell you what bliss it would give me if you would only allow this little charmer to take his proper place, instead of the wretched substitute I so much envied yesterday. I am quite sure it would give you as much pleasure as it would me." And at the same time, while I supported her with one arm round her waist, I placed her hand upon the object to which I drew her attention, and which, throbbing fiercely, lay extended along my thigh. Emboldened by her allowing her hand to remain upon it, I unbuttoned a few buttons and removed my shirt, when out it started stiff and erect as a piece of ivory. When I again placed her hand upon it, I felt it grasped with convulsive eagerness. Excited beyond measure by this, I slipped my hand under her dress, bringing it up along her thighs until it reached the object of my adoration, and gently insinuated a finger within its moist lips.

The touch of my finger, however, within such a sensitive spot seemed to rouse her at once, for she started up, saying, "Not now, Frank, not now, dearest. You must let me go. I must have time to think over this. I know you won't refuse me when I tell you I cannot remain with you at present. There, that is a good boy, go back to the drawing room, and I shall follow you immediately." At the same time she gave a fond pressure on the sensitive plant she still held in her grasp, imprinted a warm kiss on my lips, and then tore herself from my arms.

I felt that the place was not such as to enable me to attempt to carry the matter farther at present, and delaying for a minute or two in the conservatory that I might calm down my excitement a little, I slipped quietly back to the drawing room. To cover the agitation I still felt, I again joined in the waltz with the first partner I could find. In a few minutes Laura returned to the room, nor could anyone have possibly discovered from her manner that she had so recently undergone such violent emotion. I could hardly believe it possible that the seemingly proud and haughty girl was the same panting, trembling creature who had so recently been in my arms.

I soon, however, found reason to regret I had not chosen a more fitting reason for my denouement, in which case I might perhaps have turned it to greater profit than I appeared likely to do. With the morning, she had recovered all her coolness and self-possession, and had evidently determined on the course she was to pursue. She did not leave her room till breakfast time, and afterwards evaded all my stratagems to obtain a private interview with her.

After luncheon the horses were brought to the door, and a large party started out for a ride. When we had gone a short distance, she contrived to let the others get ahead of us, so as to leave us alone together, for I had got her to dispense with Master John's attendance when I accompanied her. She then turned up a quiet lane which led to a common where there was little chance of our meeting anyone, and where the many bushes, scattered in large clumps over it, were high enough to conceal us from observation.

Then, without any hesitation, she entered at once on the subject which engrossed all my thoughts. She said she could not imagine how I could possibly have discovered her secret, but that as it was clear I had done so, it was no use for her now to attempt to deny it, and that she was quite sure I would not make any use of it that could be injurious to her.

"But don't suppose," said she, "that I am offended at the manner you took of showing me you had found out my propensity. It was a very good idea, and I shall be delighted to become better acquainted with my new friend," at the same time placing her hand upon him. "He is a very handsome little fellow, but I must tell you frankly that though I shall be happy to contribute as far as I safely can to afford him amusement, you must not expect that I can allow him to do what might get me into most serious difficulties. Perhaps after a time even this may be managed, but at present it is out of the question, so he must be contented for the present with the pleasures I can safely afford him."

As she spoke, she continued to unbutton my trousers and remove my shirt, until she had fairly uncovered her new acquaintance, which started out under the pressure of her soft fingers showing his head proudly erect. She loaded it with caresses, at the same time expressing in the warmest terms her admiration of its size and beauty. I saw at once from her manner that she had made her mind up on the subject and that there was no chance of complete success on that occasion at least. So I resolved to make the best of the opportunity and humour her inclination, and do all in my power to gratify her in her own way, trusting that on some more propitious occasion I might obtain my wishes in their fullest extent.

Ascertaining, therefore, that there was no one in sight and that we were in such a position as to be able to command a view all round of some considerable distance so that no one could approach us without being observed, I said that all I desired was to contribute to her happiness, and that I only wanted to know in what manner that could be best done, and that I was quite ready to use every exertion in my power to effect it; that if she had any curiosity about her new acquaintance, I was quite prepared to do anything I could to gratify her. She said she was curious about it, and would be delighted to have a better view of it and see what it could do.

I immediately unbuttoned my braces and let down my trousers and tucked up my shirt under my waistcoat, then, bringing my leg over the horse so as to sit on one side in her own fashion, exposed everything to her view. She seemed perfectly enchanted as she took hold of and played with the ivory column and uncovered its ruby head and explored the secrets of the pendant receptacles of the liquid of life. She seemed to be fully aware of the effect of her soft hand moving up and down upon the object of her worship, and she watched with eagerness the consequences her operation produced. I did not attempt to conceal my emotions from her in the least, and gave myself up to the voluptuous sensations which her proceedings could not fail to occasion, till they attained such a height that a full overflow of the precious liquid, spouting from the overexcited tube, fairly attested the effect produced upon me. She gazed upon the charming sight with evident delight, and dwelt upon every excited motion I made, endeavouring by every means in her power to heighten and increase my enjoyment.

When I had in some measure recovered from the pleasure-trance, I threw my arms around her and thanked her for all the pleasure she had afforded me and said it was not fair that I should enjoy all the delight, and I trusted she would allow me to repeat upon her the lesson she had thus practised on me. She said at once that she would not get off the horse, but that if it would afford me any pleasure she was quite willing that I should do anything I liked with her in that position. I saw it was no use to attempt more, so I resolved to make the most of my situation.

Dismounting from my horse, I removed her leg from the horn of the saddle, and raising up her clothes discovered her most exquisite thighs and the enchanting object between them almost completely hidden under a cluster of dark-auburn curly hair. After kissing and caressing it for some minutes, parting the moist lips, and tickling the surrounding moss, I tried to introduce my finger. The tightness of the aperture and the difficulty I had in getting it in beyond an inch or two soon satisfied me that either the pain or the fear of doing mischief had prevented her from using the substitute to such an extent as to deprive the first living entrant of the glory and pleasure of a victory over her virgin charms, and this discovery increased tenfold the desire I felt to be the conqueror in such a splendid field of battle. I did the best I could in the situation in which I was placed, and partly with my finger and partly with my tongue I succeeded in creating such a degree of titillation upon her sensitive clitoris and the adjacent parts that, sided as it was by the excitement of the scene that had previously been enacted, it produced such an effect upon her as she had never previously experienced. When her convulsive motions ceased, and the stream flowed over my fingers down her thighs, she bent down her head and fondly kissed me, acknowledging that I had contrived to afford her more pleasure than she had believed it possible she could enjoy.

I seized the opportunity to point out to her the effect which her wanton hand had upon my champion, for she had now bent down to grasp it and play with it again and it still held up its proud head as erect as ever. I endeavoured to persuade her that what she had experienced was nothing in comparison with the bliss he could bestow upon her. But she remained firm, and would not allow me to give her a practical illustration of my theory, though she was so delighted with her little friend that she continued to caress and fondle him whenever she could, almost all the way till we reached home.

Two or three scenes of this nature followed in the course of the few following days, and still I could not contrive to get further with her. I therefore resolved to try the effect of a stratagem that had occurred to me. Though she had resisted all my entreaties to meet me at the summer house, I had told her the day after our explanation that I would not act so cruelly to her as she did to me, and that I was desirous to contribute to her amusement in any manner she liked best, and, therefore, as she seemed determined that her visits to the summer house should be solitary ones, I would put some books and pictures in the hiding-place which I was sure would divert her and add to her enjoyment whenever she would take a fancy to repair thither. I kept a watch upon her, but never could catch her there, though I soon became aware from the change in the position of the books that she occasionally visited the place when she knew I was away and could not surprise her.

I selected a day on which a party was made up to visit some objects of curiosity in the neighbourhood, and when she had announced her intention to stay at home, having already been often at the place, and to allow another lady of the party to ride her horse. In the morning I arranged with my groom that he should file off the heads of the nails of one of my horse's shoes, so that the shoe should come off easily, and I appointed him to meet me a short distance from the house on the road we were to take.

After I had proceeded with the party for a few miles, I pretended to think that my horse was going lame, and dismounting, I exhibited one foot with the shoe nearly off. As the horse was a valuable one, the excuse was readily accepted that I could not proceed farther, but must walk him back quietly. As soon, however, as the party had got out of sight, by the aid of a hammer and a few nails I had taken in my pocket, I fastened the shoe, and started back at full speed. Meeting my groom at the place I had appointed, I told him to get the horse properly shod and then take him to a small inn in a retired place a few miles off, so as not to have my return known at the hall. I then hastened to make my way across the fields to the summer house, having a strong hope that Laura would take advantage of the opportunity for visiting it, as my absence would render it safe for her to do so and would at the same time preclude the chance of her being able to have any gratification in my company and reduce her to her solitary amusement.

On making a more minute inspection of the summer house, I had discovered a circumstance which was not apparent at first sight and which had inspired me with the idea of my present operation. The ceiling was formed of small branches, split and nailed together in the form of panels. One of these, I discovered, was moveable and gave access to a small apartment above, part of which was floored over and occasionally used by the gardener to dry seeds. To this apartment the only access was by means of a ladder. The ceiling however was low enough to admit of my catching hold of the sides of the opening when standing on a stool, and thus swinging myself up into the interior. I had contrived, by means of oiling the hinges well and attaching a weight with a pulley, to make the entrance open easily and without the least noise, and I had also made some small apertures in the roof from which I could keep a lookout.

I immediately took possession of my hiding place and closed the entrance, resolved to take the chance of Laura's coming if I had to wait there the whole day, for I knew the precaution I had taken would prevent anything being known of my being in the neighbourhood until the return of the party, who had made the necessary arrangements for taking refreshments with them, and were not to be back till the evening.

I waited with patience all the forenoon, comforted with the idea that in all probability Laura would find herself at leisure after luncheon, at which time some of the elder part of the company who had not joined the expedition usually drove out.

It happened as I had anticipated, and very soon after the ordinary luncheon hour I was rejoiced to see Laura approaching. I was very certain, from the manner in which she looked about her as she drew near, what her object was, and I made my arrangements before she arrived so as to be able to keep perfectly still till the proper time came. After taking a walk round the place apparently to make certain that no one was in the neighbourhood, she came in, and taking out one of the books, sat down to peruse it. Convinced that my only chance of success was to catch her in the critical moment when she would be too much overwhelmed by her voluptuous sensations to offer any resistance, and afraid that any precipitate movement on my part might enable her to retain that self-command of which she possessed so large a share, I waited quietly for the effect of the seductive entertainment I had provided for her. Nor was it long before it began to produce the expected result. Her colour heightened, she moved backwards and forwards upon the couch apparently unconsciously, and at last her fingers stole under her petticoats and reached the part which was the principal scene of her excitement and which I could see from the motions of her arm she was attempting to allay. In a few minutes she appeared to be unable longer to withstand the temptation which the opportunity offered, and rising up, she went to the hiding-place and took from it some lascivious pictures and the little object with which she intended to solace herself.

After heightening her desires by an attentive examination of the seductive plates, she raised her dress and stretched herself on the couch, much in the same attitude in which I had previously seen her, and after a little toying with her finger she separated the ruby lips and introduced the mock representation of that part of me which I was so eager to enable her to judge how much more pleasure the reality would afford her. Even then I had the patience to wait until she had made use of it for some little time and until I could discern from sundry sighs that the pleasure it was giving her was approaching a climax. Then gently raising the trap door and catching hold of the sides, I quietly let myself drop into the apartment below. A slight rustling noise I made attracted her attention, and looking up from her book, she beheld my almost naked body with the most prominent object of it standing fiercely erect, for I had let down my trousers and turned up my shirt so as to afford her a complete view of my person.

At this sight, so suddenly and unexpectedly presented to her, without her at first being able to discover who it was that thus presented himself in such a guise, she was so struck with surprise and astonishment that she was in the utmost consternation and completely lost her presence of mind, remaining motionless even after I had fully appeared before her and approached her so that she must have recognised me. Aware that, if I was to profit by the opportunity, I must not lose a moment in explanation, I at once got between her thighs which were stretched out widely extended, and withdrawing the wretched mock article from its darling retreat, I threw myself upon her and instantly without the least hesitation replaced it with the reality. I was quite aware I should find some difficulty in getting admission, but most fortunately her situation was so extremely favourable that I was enabled so far to effect my object as to get the head of my weapon fairly inserted within the delicious lips of her charmer before she had recovered from her surprise sufficiently to offer any opposition.

LAURA MIDDLETON

Then, indeed, she attempted to rise up, exclaiming,
"Oh! Frank, Frank, this will never do." By this
time, however, I had got my arms fairly round her
waist and held her locked in a close embrace, and
while I endeavoured to stifle her remonstrances
with burning kisses on her fair lips, I exerted my
utmost efforts to improve my position. My thrusts
and heaves, driven with the greatest vigour my
burning passion could inspire me with, evidently
hurt her severely, but this I had expected and was
fully prepared for, as I was aware from my previous inspections of the charming spot that it never
had been stretched to such an extent as to enable
me to attain free admission, and consequently I
was not disposed to relax in my efforts on that account, trusting that the overwhelming pleasure that
would ensue would fully make up for all suffering,
and that I should obtain full possession, as soon as
she should be enabled to join in my transports.

Her very struggles, caused partly by pain and
partly by apprehension, as she endeavoured to rise
up, only aided me in effecting my purpose, and
after a short contest, I had the satisfaction and delight of feeling the resistance which her virgin obstacles had offered to my progress entirely give
way, and my victorious champion had penetrated
her inmost secret recesses in such an effectual manner as to produce the most delicious conjunction of
the most sensitive parts of our bodies that can possibly be conceived. The effect upon her, however,
was not so immediately delightful as it was upon
me. The pain occasioned by the last few thrusts by
which I had completed the achievement had been

so severe as to make her abandon her resistance, and when it suddenly ceased, on my weapon obtaining complete entrance, she sank back on the couch as if exhausted. I followed her example and sank down upon her, pressing her more closely in my arms, and being now relieved from the necessity of using force, I regulated the movements of my victorious champion so as to try to avoid as far as possible giving her any further pain, and endeavoured to replace it with more delightful sensations. But with the removal of the pain her apprehensions revived, and she again entreated me to let her rise. Her request, however, now came too late—even had I been disposed to comply with it, which I certainly was not, the excited state into which she had worked herself previous to my appearing on the scene had produced such an effect upon her frame that very few up-and-down movements of my pleasure-giver within the now thoroughly opened up premises were quite sufficient to remove all traces of the pain and to produce the consummation he was labouring to effect and was so eager to join in. Before she had time to repeat her request and even before I was quite prepared to respond to the tide of joy, her head again sank back and she exclaimed, "Oh! Oh! Delicious, oh! Dearest, oh! I can bear it no longer." Her extatic movements, while in the act of enjoyment, were all that was required to make me join in her delight, and pouring forth a torrent of bliss I sank motionless on her breast enjoying a happiness that may be conceived but cannot possibly be described.

When I had recovered a little from my transports, still retaining my place, I thought it was time to endeavour to appease her indignation which I feared might have been aroused at the trap I had evidently laid for her. But I soon found I had no occasion to be alarmed on this subject. She had no hesitation in admitting that, though she had so long resisted my entrance, it had only been from the fear of the consequences and she had all along been as anxious as I was for the crowning pleasure from the first moment when she had viewed the potent charms of my pleasure-giver, and she had been as much disappointed and annoyed at the unsatisfactory manner in which our intercourse had hitherto been conducted; and she even went on to say that whatever the consequences might be to her, she was rejoiced I had had the courage to make her break through the restraint she had imposed on herself.

Accordingly, when I asked her whether her new acquaintance had not justified, by the result he had produced, all that I had predicted as the consequences of his being admitted into his present delicious quarter, she frankly confessed that though she at first had suffered dreadfully from the tearing open of her interior, the final close had much more than gratified all her expectation and had fully made up for all she had endured. And she added that she never would have forgiven me, if I had yielded to her entreaties and left the performance unfinished.   ,

"But now," said she, "that this little darling has done his duty so well, do get up and take a look about, in case anyone should stray in this direction. I don't want to part with you so soon, but it would never do for anyone to come in and catch us in this situation."

"No, no, dearest," I replied, "you only half enjoyed yourself the last time, and I am afraid if I were to withdraw this little gentleman I might have to give you more pain in replacing him, and as I want you thoroughly to enter into all the blissful sensations of this occasion, you must let him remain where he is."

"What," said she, "do you mean to say he can do it again? Oh! That would be delicious! But I am so frightened for anyone coming."

"Well, dearest, just keep your arms round me, and I shall raise you up till we can take a look about us." And clasping her round the waist so as to keep us still firmly united by the pleasantest of all links, I raised her up to a position from which we could command a view all round us, and thus satisfy ourselves that all was safe.

Then gently laying her down, I again commenced operations; at first thrusting my weapon cautiously and gradually in and out of the charming orifice so as to avoid the risk of hurting her. But I soon found there was no danger of this. The elements of pleasure were so fiercely aroused within her that my exertions occasioned very different sensations from those which had accompanied my first entrance into her delicious quarters, and in a few minutes her efforts to promote our mutual bliss vied with, if they did not exceed, my own. For the first time in her life she thoroughly enjoyed the most exquisite of all sensations a woman can be

blessed with, that of having her most sensitive region fully gorged with the masterpiece which first
works her up to the most amorous frenzy and then
subdues her by making her die away with itself
in melting bliss. There was not a moment from the
time when I half withdrew and again inserted the
delicious morsel, the possession of which she so
much enjoyed, till the overwhelming bliss of mutual emission took away our senses, that she did
not evince both by her gestures and her words the
most excessive and frantic delight, and I need
hardly say that my enjoyment equalled hers.

When our second course was finished, I withdrew my still unexhausted weapon, which notwithstanding its double victory still held up its
head bravely, but I was somewhat horrified at the
mingled tide which now poured out its crimson
stream down her thighs. She was in great distress
less it might betray her, but I managed to prevent
any of it getting upon her dress and persuaded her
to accompany me to a small fountain a little way
off where, dipping my handkerchief in the water,
I first removed all marks of the conflict, and then
continued to bathe the swollen and tender lips
which still bore traces of the fierce nature of the
combat. Finding the cooling sensation was grateful
to her, I continued the application until the sight
of her charms, thus freely exposed, made the author
of the mischief so wild at the contemplation of
the effects of his own deeds that I was obliged to
show the state he was in, and tell her that it would
require another defeat before he could be quited.
She hesitated a little from the fear of the pain ac-

companying his re-entrance in the present tender state of her interior. But seeing that he also bore bloody marks of the fray, she insisted on reciprocating the good offices I had bestowed upon her, and taking the handkerchief, she proceeded to remove them by tenderly bathing the little gentleman.

Pretty well aware what would be the consequence of this proceeding, I allowed her to take her own way. And as even the application of the cold water failed to quench his ardour, she at length admitted that there was nothing for it but to renew the combat and we accordingly returned to the summer house.

Notwithstanding all my care, the pain I occasioned her while getting fairly established within her was very severe; but she persevered in her efforts to introduce him to his old quarters until she had effectually accomplished it to our mutual satisfaction. As soon as I had fairly reached the bottom, I desisted from the attack, and allowed her to remain quiet till all her suffering had entirely subsided and she was again in a condition to be able to enjoy the perfect pleasure.

The first hot eagerness of novelty being now over, we both felt disposed on this occasion to prolong our enjoyment as much as possible and we accordingly proceeded with the operation more leisurely, watching the effects to our mutual efforts to produce the greatest enjoyment, and telling each other when to quicken or retard our movements, so as to keep the delicious sensations at their highest pitch, and at the same time delay the final crisis as long as possible. Sometimes it was I who would urge the fierce intruder backwards and forwards in his career of pleasure; and sometimes, making me remain still, it was she who, with up-and-down heaves of her delicious buttocks, would make the lips and sides of her charming, tight-fitting sheath move over my entranced weapon, creating within it the most voluptuous sensations it is possible to conceive. But at length we could restrain ourselves no longer, and then again commenced a furious struggle of mutual heaves and thrusts intermingled with burning kisses and fond caresses, which soon resulted in drawing from us a pleasing stream of such enchanting extasy that Laura declared it was even more delicious than the previous one, which she had believed could not have been surpassed.

By this time she began to be afraid that her absence might be noticed and insisted that it was time for her to return to the hall. Before she left me I easily persuaded her to resume her morning visits to the summer house, and to allow me to meet her there. I satisfied her that there was no risk in this, as in the event of anyone coming to the place by chance, I could easily take refuge in my hiding-place so that no suspicion could arise if she were found there alone.

For several mornings we continued to indulge ourselves with a repetition of our amorous pranks and every meeting only added to the zest with which we gave ourselves up to every mode of enjoyment we could devise.

The sole drawback to our pleasures was the

impossibility in such an exposed situation of enjoying the sight and the touch at once of the whole of each other's charms, and I anxiously watched for any opportunity when we might be able to accomplish this. One forenoon Lady Middleton had accompanied the rest of the party on a visit to some friends in the neighbourhood from which they were not to return till night, leaving at home only Sir Hugh, Miss Middleton, Laura, and myself. I had made some excuse for not accompanying the party, but my real reason was the wish to have an opportunity of meeting Laura, as she had been unable to keep her appointment with me that morning, though I little expected that I was to be thereby enabled to arrange for the full accomplishment of our most anxious wishes.

I was sitting with the two ladies when a servant brought in a note for Miss Middleton saying that the messenger waited for an answer. She read it and said to Laura, "This is very provoking, it is a note from Mr. Percival asking me to come over and meet the Savilles at dinner. I should like so much to go, as all our party are away to-day, and I shall not have another opportunity of meeting my old friends; but I am afraid there is no conveyance to take me. If the pony were able to go, I should drive over in the pony-chaise, but I fear he is not sufficiently recovered from his accident."

Laura's eyes and mine met, and all the advantage of getting her aunt away for the night flashed upon us. I gave her a look to urge her aunt to go. She reflected for a minute, and then said she did not think the pony was fit for work yet, but that her aunt might send for a carriage from the town, which was some miles distant, and that she would arrange with her mother to come for her the next morning.

To this, however, Miss Middleton objected, saying that before a messenger could go on foot and bring the carriage it would be too late, even if he succeeded in getting it, which was doubtful.

I now thought I might venture to interfere, and addressing Miss Middleton I said, "I did not think you would have treated me with so much ceremony. You know there are two horses of mine standing idle in the stable which are quite at your service; if you wish to send a messenger into town, my servant shall go directly, but I think the best plan will be for you to allow me to drive you over in my dogcart, and as you may not like coming home in the dark, I shall come back for you to-morrow at any hour you may fix." She appeared to hesitate, but Laura had little difficulty in persuading her to accept my offer. She accordingly went to prepare, while I ordered the dogcart to be got ready. Before setting out I arranged with Laura that as it might appear strange were I to insist on returning to dinner when she was alone at home with her father, I should, if invited, remain at the Percivals till evening. She agreed to go to bed at her usual hour and to leave the door connecting her room and mine unlocked and to tie a white ribbon to the door-handle, if all was safe for me to come to her. I started with Miss Middleton, and as I had expected was urged to remain till next day. I at once agreed to stay for dinner, but refused all their pressing to remain all night on the plea that I had made no preparations for so doing. I remained till pretty late and then started for the Hall, promising to return the next forenoon for Miss Middleton.

By the time I arrived everyone had gone to bed, and I hastened to follow their example.

My first impulse was to examine Laura's door, and I was rejoiced to find the agreed-on signal. I hastily stripped off my clothes, and opening the door softly, found her still awake, awaiting my arrival. Throwing down the bed clothes I was about to jump into her arms, when it occurred to me that the operations we contemplated might perhaps leave some traces behind, which might lead to suspicion if discovered in her bed. I therefore said to her that it would be safer for her to repair with me to mine. Ascertaining that her door was locked so as to prevent all intrusion, I took her round the waist and led her to my room.

As soon as we reached the bedside I threw off my shirt and said, "Now, dearest, since we have at last obtained the long desired opportunity we must endeavour to avail ourselves of it to the best of our abilities. I shall try to contribute as much as I can to your happiness and I am sure you will not hesitate to do anything in your power to add to mine. Now, the first thing to be done is to get rid of all these obstacles to my fully seeing and enjoying all your charms."

She made no objection to my removing the envious veil which covered her person. Indeed I think she was quite as anxious as I was to enjoy the delight which the contemplation of each other's beauties was sure to produce upon us. However, at last we were both too eager to enjoy the *summum bonum* of earthly felicity to give up much time to the preliminaries.

After a cursory inspection of each other's persons, I stretched her at full length upon the bed and getting upon her I made her herself insert my stiffly distended champion into her delicious pleasure-sheath, and enabled her for the first time to enjoy the delicious sensation occasioned by the complete contact in every quarter of our naked bodies. Making her clasp her arms around me, and twist her thighs and legs about my hips, I drove my rammer into her as far as it would go and then commenced a more voluptuous encounter than any we had yet sustained. Fired by the sight she had enjoyed of my naked person and animated by the delicious sensations which our close contact was sure to occasion, she responded at once to all my movements and there ensued a fierce combat between us, each of us striving by every artifice and exertion in our power to prove the victor, and while conquering, to add to the enjoyment of the vanquished. She proved the conqueror by forcing me to be the first to yield up my tribute; but not wishing to be outdone in the capacity of conferring pleasure, I continued my vigorous heaves and thrusts in the delicious receptacle in which I was engulphed, while I felt the warm life-drops bursting from me in a torrent of bliss, until I was sensible that she also had yielded to the potent spell and shared my enjoyment by mingling her contribu-

tion with the tide which flowed from me. Then
with a warm kiss we ceased our efforts and lay for
a while locked in each other's arms, still joined together by the tender tie that bound us in a perfect
heaven of luxurious delight.

If we could have reckoned upon a similar enjoyment every night, we would both have remained
thus closely embracing for the whole night without desiring greater pleasure.

But the slight view of her splendid charms I had
already enjoyed had only heightened my desire for
a more minute inspection of them, and I could not
afford to lose the opportunity thus fortunately
presented to me. Getting up, therefore, and light-
ing some additional candles I had prepared for the
purpose, I stretched her out all naked as she was
on the bed and commenced a thorough examination of all those beauties which I had so eagerly
longed to inspect, and which as yet I had only
been able partially and cursorily to investigate. No
part of her escaped my ardent gaze and eager touch.
She willingly yielded to my wishes, nay, she even
seemed gratified by my eagerness, and placed herself in every position in which she fancied I should
be able to detect a new beauty. Every portion of
her body, both before and behind, was in succes-
sion the object of my adoration and was covered
with the most passionate and thrilling kisses and
caresses. The effect of this may easily be imagined,
and it was not long before the imposing majesty
of my overjoyed pleasure-giver showed to her,
and equally convinced me, of the necessity we were
under of cooling our ardour by a repetition of the

same delightful process which we had already undergone.

After this was happily concluded, she insisted on having in her turn the same privilege I had enjoyed, and she made me undergo the same minute investigation to which she had been subjected. Her curiosity was excessive; every object underwent the most searching examination and of course all those parts in which there was a difference between us were more particularly and vigorously explored and discussed. It was impossible for me to remain insensible to her lascivious caresses which again roused the fire within me. My staff of love started up proud and erect as if eager to exhibit its full proportions to her ardent gaze. Upon me the effect was most delicious. To find myself lying there stark naked before a lovely girl and undergoing the delightful touches with which she covered every part of my person as she explored my most secret charms, and at the same time to gaze on all her splendid beauties which were as freely exposed before me, was bliss indeed which roused me to the highest pitch of excitement, and again I repaid her in the most delicious manner for all the pleasing sensations her charming researches had excited in me. After this we lay for some time in each other's arms luxuriating in the blissful feelings caused by our complete conjunction, till morning beginning to appear, I suggested that she should endeavour to obtain a little repose to prevent the fatigues of the night exhibiting their traces upon her too obviously the next day. Not yet satisfied, however, she laid her hand on the weapon of love, as if to ascertain whether it was yet capable of again conferring upon her the bliss she desired. Quite understanding and appreciating her object, I soon satisfied her in the most practical manner that his powers were by no means wholly exhausted, and having achieved another victory over our raging desires, we at length fell asleep locked in each other's arms.

When I awoke, the sun was shining brightly into the room. During her sleep Laura had somewhat changed her position, and instead of fronting me, had turned upon her left side, presenting her splendid posteriors to me, between which my champion was nestling himself. Judging by his imposing appearance, his powers did not seem in any way impaired by the exertions of the previous night. Turning down the bed-clothes, I for some time quietly revelled in the sight of her charms, and then getting excited beyond endurance, though unwilling to disturb her peaceful slumber, I thought I might perhaps be able without awakening her to take up a more satisfactory position than the one I enjoyed. So gently raising her right leg and creeping as close behind her as I could, I placed my right leg between her thighs in such a manner that my champion shoved himself between her legs, stretching up almost to her navel, In this position I lay for some little time till some half muttered words and certain movements of her body made me suspect that Laura in her sleep was acting over again the scenes of the previous night. Convinced that she would have no more objection than myself to the illusion being converted into the reality, I gently separated the lips of the seat of pleasure and inserted the tip of the appropriate organ. His sweet touch in such a sensitive spot at once broke her slumber. She opened her eyes, and glancing downward got a full view of my stiffly distended weapon with its ruby head quite uncovered just entering within the charming precincts of her lovely retreat, and she said smiling that it was just what she had been dreaming of. She was then going to turn herself round towards me, but I told her to remain as she was and that I thought we should be able to accomplish our wishes in that position. I pointed out to her that although we could not so well enjoy the pleasure of kissing each other, we could at least better watch and observe each other's operations while my weapon was perforating her, as the reflexion of our figures in a large mirror, which I had purposely placed so as to produce the best effect, would add greatly to our enjoyment. Looking towards it, she blushed deeply at beholding exposed to her full view her own lovely face, exquisite swelling breasts, snow-white belly and ivory thighs, with the upper part of the mount of pleasure beautifully shaded with its appropriate fringe and the lips swollen and distended with the shaft of love, while my leg, holding her thighs apart, exposed to view between them the pleasure-yielding receptacles of its liquid treasures, and at every heave I gave exhibited at full length the staff of my weapon as I alternately penetrated and then partly withdrew it from its delicious sheath. This exquisite site delighted us so much that we determined to prolong it as much as possible, and regulating each other's movements so as to keep up the enjoyment to the uttermost and at the same time hold back the crisis, we lay in the most extatic bliss for upwards of an hour, enjoying the thrilling delight which this perfect combination of the most exquisite sensations of touch and sight can confer. At length, in spite of our endeavours, we could no longer restrain the tide of passion, a few furious heaves of my maddened and thrusting pleasure-giver completed our bliss, and the genial shower sprinkled the field of pleasure and calmed our overexcited senses.

One other soul-stirring enjoyment was all we had time to accomplish before the approach of the hour at which Laura was usually called warned us that we must separate, and with the most poignant regret that we might not have another opportunity of again enjoying ourselves in such a delightful manner, we parted.

In the forenoon I drove out for Miss Middleton. As her friends wished her to remain, I of course endeavoured to persuade her to do so and offered to come back for her on any day she might fix, but she insisted on returning home that day. I had, however, the satisfaction of finding that she had made an arrangement with the friends whom she had gone to meet to pay them a visit for some weeks as soon as they returned to their own abode, which they were to do in about a week.

One circumstance, however, occurred the same day which rather counterbalanced the pleasure with which I received this intelligence. Young Master Frank on leaving school had gone to pay a visit to a school-fellow, but a letter had arrived from him that morning to say that he would be home the next day. Now his arrival and consequent occupation of the room between Laura's and mine threatened to prevent the constant agreeable intercourse which I had expected to be able to keep up with her during her aunt's absence.

I felt very much annoyed at the idea, and urged her, if possible, to get some arrangement made by which he might occupy some other apartment. She said, however, that she was afraid to make any such proposal to her mother for fear of exciting suspicions as to her object, or of occasioning my removal to another room, which would be equally destructive for our projects.

On the whole she took the matter so quietly and coolly that I was rather astonished, considering the enjoyment she evidently had in our intercourse. A little annoyed at this, I made up my mind that if my young friend retained any portion of the youthful beauty I remembered him to possess, I would endeavour if possible to make up in his arms for the enjoyment he would deprive me of by keeping me out of his sister's.

His first appearance at once decided me to follow out the idea that had occurred to me. Some years younger than his sister and just of that delightful age when the passions of manhood have begun to exert their influence on the senses but before they have taken away the attractive and charming bloom and graces of youth, he was, if possible, more captivating than his sister. Indeed, when upon one occasion I dressed him up as a girl, it was almost impossible to distinguish between them and he might easily have passed for her even among her intimate acquaintances. We became good friends at once. When the ladies left the table after dinner, I made a sign to him to come over beside me, and he was very soon communicating to me all his secrets. I easily led him to talk of his school-fellows and their amusements, and when the party rose to join the ladies he was in the midst of the details of the history of one of the elder boys to whom a married lady had taken a fancy at a house where he had been visiting, and who had conferred a favour on him of which it was very evident my young friend was somewhat envious. When we went to the drawing room, he wanted to continue the history, but I said to him that it would be better not to do so there, but that as he slept in the next room to mine, he might come to me after we had retired for the night, when we would have a better opportunity for discussing the subject. He said he would, but that I was not to expect him till everyone had gone to bed, in case his mother or sister should come into his room. Although a little surprised at this allusion to the latter, I was quite satisfied from what he said that all was right, as, unless he somewhat comprehended my object, he would not have thought it necessary to make any mystery or take any precaution on the subject.

I went to bed, and taking a book, remained awake reading until I heard my door open, and my young friend entered with only his nightshirt on. When he came to the bedside I at once threw down the bed-clothes and made room for him beside me. He jumped in instantly, and clasping him in my arms I pressed him to my bosom. He warmly returned my embrace, and the idea I had formed as to his appreciating my intentions was immediately confirmed by my finding something hard and stiff pressing against my belly, and I soon managed to ascertain that his instrument was in a state of fierce erection. After a few kisses and caresses, I led to the subject of his young friend and the lady, asking how old he was, and then laying my hand upon his organ of pleasure, asked him whether his friend's plaything was bigger than this. He said at once it was, and then taking hold of mine, which as may be supposed was standing stiff enough, he added that it was not so big as mine. Continuing to caress his little charmer, I said I was afraid it was a very naughty little gentleman, and asked whether he had ever had a lady to teach him how to behave himself properly. He said, "Oh! no! I have not been so fortunate, but I do wish I could get someone to do it with me. I can think of nothing else night or day, and I shall go wild unless I can manage it before long."

The manner in which my caresses affected him showed plainly how excitable he was. He pressed me to him, and as I grasped his instrument he twisted himself backwards and forwards endeavouring to make my hand serve as a substitute for what he so eagerly desired, while he begged of me to tell him whether I could not put him in the way of obtaining the fulfillment of his wishes. I at once promised that if he would get permission to pay me a visit at the Hall, I would arrange that he should have as much of it as he liked, if he would only allow me to witness and participate with him in his pleasures. In his delight and gratitude he at once said that he would do anything I liked, that I had only to tell what I wanted and he would be as eager as I could be to do whatever was in his power that would contribute to my enjoyment.

During this conversation I had been playing with his pretty little instrument as he had been with mine, and I had occasionally introduced it between my thighs squeezing them together so as to compress it between them and meeting and returning the thrusts which he could not help giving on finding his little charmer so agreeably tickled by my soft flesh. This drew from him exclamations of delight.

"Why, my dear boy," said I, "if this gives you pleasure, as I imagine it does, I think I could manage to make you do it in a manner that will be more agreeable still." Turning round to him I presented to him my posteriors, and retaining hold of his instrument I inserted it between my hips, and squeezing and pressing it in the same manner as formerly, I enabled him to enjoy the pleasing friction over a larger portion of the surface of his now inflamed weapon. This seemed to gratify him extremely, and he repeatedly thanked me for the nice way in which he said I made him do it, and protested that he had never enjoyed it so much before. I told him I thought I could make it even pleasanter still. I had still retained my fingers round the root of his sensitive plant, and I now drew it back a little, and raising the point, directed it to the orifice between the cheeks of my posteriors. Opening the lips so as to permit the head to penetrate a short way, I made the cheeks of my bottom close round the head of the intruder so as to produce a most delicious compression upon it, which drew from him the exclamation, "Oh! This is splendid!"

I then asked him whether he had ever put it in here before. He seemed a little surprised at the question, and said, "No," and then putting down his hand and ascertaining the little charmer's head was actually within the lips of the orifice, he immediately asked, "Will it go in?"

"Just try, my dear boy," was my answer.

He did not wait for any pressing, but immediately pressed forwards, and as I favoured the insertion as much as I could, a very few thrusts sufficed to lodge the charming intruder fairly within me, evidently as much to his delight as it was to mine. As soon as it was driven completely home, and his thighs and belly came in close contact with my buttocks, he ceased his movements and lay still for some minutes, apparently in the greatest extasy. The complete constriction which was thus established on every part of his stiff-standing instrument—so tightly fitting and pressing upon it and yet so deliciously tender and soft —was so different from anything he had ever previously felt, when his own or a school-fellow's hand had procured for him an emission, it seemed quite to overpower him.

After fully enjoying himself for a little time, he withdrew the inflamed morsel which I felt burning hot within me, bringing it out nearly to its full extent and then replacing it.

He then said, "Tell me, my dear fellow, may I do this, it is so delicious, but I am afraid of hurting you."

"Hurting me?" I replied. "You need not be very afraid of that. Does that feel as if you were hurting me," taking his hand and placing it upon my inflamed member of which in his excitement he had lost his hold, and which throbbing and burning stood up fiercely erected along my belly, excited to the utmost by the charming pressure which his member exerted upon its sensitive root. "No, no, the little charmer is not quite big enough yet to do any harm, he is just the size to give me as much pleasure as he will give you. So don't be afraid to do anything you like, and I shall do my best to help you!"

Encouraged by this, he commenced operations which I seconded with all my might. At first he pushed backwards and forwards, gently and regularly, and I had no difficulty in keeping time with him, but after a little he became so excited and thrust followed thrust with such velocity and so irregularly that I found it quite impossible to keep in unison with him, and could only aid his frantic efforts by the compression of the muscles upon his raging champion, which I exerted whenever he gave me an opportunity by making a more prolonged thrust than usual within me. In the meantime his panting sobs and sighs bore testimony to the excess of his enjoyment and the near approach of the voluptuous crisis, which was speedily announced by an exclamation, "Oh, goodness, oh!" I felt my delightful invader pressed into me with all his force, as if he wished his whole body could follow. I endeavoured to add to his delight by a few movements on my part, for he was now so overcome with pleasure as to be almost incapable of motion, and contracting the mouth of the orifice as much as I could, I pressed upon his swollen and throbbing column and strove to prolong his pleasure by delaying as long as possible the passage of the precious liquid through it, which was now bursting from him in furious jets. I succeeded in this so well that he has often told me since that in all the amorous encounters he has subsequently been engaged in, and they are not a few, he has never enjoyed such delicious sensations as he did on this occasion when he first felt the ravishing delight of his pleasure-giving member being completely engulphed within, and compressed by, the magical circle of living flesh.

After he had lain quiet for a little while, I felt his somewhat attenuated weapon slip out of me. He then turned himself round, presenting his buttocks to me and, still keeping his hold on my member which he had maintained during all his raptures, he gently drew me round also, nothing unwilling, and presenting his captive at the entrance to its destined prison, he opened the lips of his orifice as much as he could, and tried to get him in.

I was amused and delighted with his eagerness

about it, but fearful of hurting him, I did not attempt to force my way in, until he asked me why I did not assist him in getting it farther in. I said simply because I was afraid that, as he had not tried it before, I might hurt him the first time, but that if he would allow me to try, I would endeavour to do it with as little suffering to him as possible. He at once told me to do anything I liked, that he could not expect me to allow him to enjoy himself within me again unless he reciprocated the pleasure and that he would willingly suffer any amount of pain to be permitted again to taste the delight he had already felt. I was in no way averse to take him at his word and accordingly set to work. As he gave me every facility, I was enabled with the aid of a little cold cream to make my way in with less difficulty than I had expected. My first penetration no doubt hurt him a little, but he bore it manfully and urged me to proceed till, to my infinite delight, I was fairly lodged within him up to the hilt. The avenue was as tight and delightful as possible, but it was of that charming elasticity which yielded sufficiently to admit the invader, and at the same time pressed upon him with that degree of force which occasioned the most consummate voluptuous gratifications. As soon as I was fairly in, all annoyance seemed fairly at an end and, judging from the rise of his thermometer which I held in my hand, there succeeded an increase of the pleasure heat which I had hardly anticipated. The result was that eagerly availing himself of the lessons I had given him, he set to work so deliciously and exerted himself so much to promote my pleasure that in spite of my efforts to prolong the enjoyment, he drew down from me in a very few minutes the first flow that had saturated his virgin premises.

After some little fondling of each other he again wished to repeat the operation. I told him I was afraid of his exerting himself too much, and proposed that we should put it off till morning, but he would not be satisfied with this, and urged me to comply by appealing to an argument the strength and beauty of which I could not withstand. Again this fascinating charmer was plunged into my interior with the same lascivious results and again I was rewarded for my compliance by the full enjoyment of his delicious charms, and after we had each thus attained again to the height of felicity we fell asleep locked in a close embrace.

I awoke early in the morning before he did, and I delighted myself with a view of all his naked charms while he still slumbered. I was unwilling to awaken him even to satisfy my own raging desires inflamed by the sight of such beauty, for I saw that his lovely champion was already raising his head proudly aloft, as fiercely as if he had not undergone any fatigue on the previous night, and I was convinced that if he once awoke, nothing would prevent him from at once commencing and continuing the delightful game till it was time to appear at breakfast.

I therefore resolved to keep quiet as long as possible, and creeping gently as close to him as I could, I placed my throbbing weapon in the hollow between his buttocks, and in that delicious position remained quiet until he awoke. When he did open his eyes, he turned his head round, and finding how he was situated and that I had been awake for some time, he scolded me for wasting so much valuable time, and while he took hold of and insinuated my pleasure-giver into the appropriate niche with which it was in such close contact, he vowed that he was much disposed to punish me by not allowing him to enter.

The joys of the previous evening were repeated. He in his turn penetrated into my interior, and revelled in the same lascivious enjoyment. After we had each thus allayed our fires a little by a copious discharge, we proceeded to a minute examination of our respective persons, while I was highly delighted with the unrestrained exhibition of such charms as have seldom fallen under my notice.

I found that he was no less struck and pleased with what I in return placed at his disposal. Anything of the kind he had previously seen had been of boys of his own age, and this merely by stealth when he had no opportunity of making minute observations. My somewhat more mature proportions, occasioned by the difference of a few years in our ages, were therefore fully appreciated and drew from him the warmest encomiums and the most luxurious caresses.

While Frank and I were thus agreeably occupied in a minute investigation of each other's charms, I reverted to what had fallen from him the previous evening, and asked if he really meant to say that his sister was in the habit of visiting him after he had gone to bed.

"Not now," he replied, "I only wish she did, and I would soon repay her the lessons she used to give me. Do you know it was she who first taught me how to do anything in this way?"

I expressed my surprise and curiosity to know what had occurred between them, and he at once proceeded to enlighten me, saying that from the kindness I had shown him he was sure he need have no reserve with me.

"It was," he said, "about eighteen months ago, when she had returned from school, that our first amusement began. We then slept in the same rooms we now occupy, and as some of my younger brothers were in the room where you are, I used often to lock the door at night to prevent them from coming in and tormenting me. Laura used generally to come to bed before her aunt. She somehow ascertained that I shut myself up in my room and probably imagined that I was better informed on certain subjects than I really was.

"One evening on which there were some old people at dinner who were likely to occupy our aunt's attention and keep her up late, Laura said to me that she was tired of the party in the drawing room, but that she was not inclined to sleep, and that if I left the door open between our rooms she would come and sit with me for a while. I sat up for some time, expecting to hear her come to her room, but at length I grew tired of waiting, undressed, and went to bed. I suspected she must have crept softly to her own room and waited there without my being aware of it till this took place, for I had hardly got into bed and put out the candle when I heard her come in. She came to the bedside and inquired in a low voice if I was awake. On my answering her, she said we had better not talk loud in case of disturbing the young people in the next room. She sat down by the bedside and leaned over me, putting an arm round my neck and kissing me warmly. Then, putting her hand under the bed-clothes, she began to caress my naked bosom. This seemed a little strange to me, but very pleasant. And it was still more agreeable when, putting my arm round her neck, I found that she also was undressed and had nothing but her nightshift and a dressing gown which was quite open at the front. This she accounted for by saying she must be ready to slip into bed if she heard her aunt coming.

"The touch of her naked breasts, which were then just beginning to acquire their full, round form, quite delighted me, and it was while playing with them that the first voluptuous sensations were awakened within me. I had previously been sometimes surprised, especially on awakening in the morning, to find a certain little gentleman quite hard and stiff, and had been at a loss to ascertain what was the cause. And I was now still more surprised that as I played with her soft, yielding globes, the same effect occurred, but although the sensation was most agreeable, I was too ignorant regarding such matters to be able to connect the cause with the effect. Laura continued to kiss and play with me for some time, and at last I became aware that while with one hand she caressed me, the other was employed in some movement about her own person, the object of which I did not understand and did not think of investigating. The effect, however, seemed to be pleasant to her, for her kisses and caresses increased in ardour till at last with a heavy sigh they ceased at once; and she remained for a few minutes perfectly still. Then after another kiss she said she was afraid her aunt might come and find her away. So making me promise to say nothing of her visit she left me.

"Our interview had been so agreeable to me that I pressed her to renew it on the succeeding night, which she willingly agreed to do, and somewhat of the same procedure occurred on that and several subsequent occasions. I gradually began to discover that as her caresses increased and as her hand came to wander lower down on my person the effect which was produced upon a certain part came to increase in force and to be accompanied with more pleasant sensations. This aroused a suspicion in my mind that there must be some connection between them. So one night, when my little plaything was particularly stiff, and she was very much excited, I took her hand which had never before strayed below my navel and, certainly by no means unwillingly on her part, drew it down and placed it on the throbbing object that had raised my curiosity. She made not the least objection to my making her grasp it, and after handling it for a little, she asked me what was the meaning of it and what I wanted her to do with it. I said I did not know, but that I suspected she knew better than I did, as it was only when she played with me that it became in its present state. She laughed and asked me if it gave me any pleasure for her to play with it. I told her it did, and begged of her to continue to fondle it. She complied very willingly, and then began to question me how long it was since it had commenced to get into this state and whether I had every played with it myself, or done anything to procure myself pleasure with it. I told her that it was only of late that it had often been in the way of getting stiff, and explained how much it had been affected by her caresses. She then said she thought she might perhaps be able to procure for me still greater pleasure with it, but that it would take a little time to do so, and as she could not remain long enough that night she would come back and try what she could do on the first favourable opportunity.

"The next evening she complained of a headache and retired to bed earlier than usual. As soon as she came into my room, she lighted my candle, stripped down the bed-clothes, made me take off my nightshirt, and at once began to amuse herself with my little plaything. It swelled out and increased in size under her playful fondling to an extent that surprised me. After she had satisfied her curiosity respecting it and its appendages by a strict examination of every part, she took it in her hand and began to rub it up and down. She then put out the candle, so that I did not see what was probably the case—while endeavouring to procure me pleasure, she was at the same time operating upon herself for the same agreeable purpose. I certainly very much enjoyed her performance upon my sensitive article, but still I felt as if something was wanting, and I was greatly disappointed when as as usual she sunk almost fainting on my bosom and ceased her efforts.

"After a little she recovered herself and said she was afraid I was still too young to be able to enjoy the full pleasure of what she had been doing, but that she would try again the following night. Still two or three nights passed without anything occurring to heighten my enjoyment.

"By this time I had begun to express some curiosity with regard to her person and to wish to be allowed to extend my researches over it as freely as her hands roved over mine. With some little difficulty I prevailed on her to remove her dressing gown and nightshift and stretch herself naked on the bed beside me. I had been aware from what I had seen of some little girls that there was a considerable difference in our formation, but I was astonished at first on finding her centre-part so thickly shaded with hair. I quite delighted with its beauty, was soon tempted to get my fingers between the moist ruby lips of the charming little slit which I discovered within the curly forest, and to begin to explore its recesses. The sensitive little organ I found within so closely resembling, though on a smaller scale, my own organ of pleasure, did not escape my observation, as wakened up by my lascivious touches it darted its little head out from its hiding-place. It was not long before I discovered that this invasion of her inmost recesses occasioned Laura the greatest delight. She seemed at first to hesitate a little, but summing up courage she took hold of my hand and, inserting my fingers within the warmly moist cavity, made me move it up and down within her. At the same time she grasped my weapon and rubbed it backwards and forwards more rapidly and more forcibly than she had ever done before. I felt greatly excited and continued the titillating movements of my finger within her with the greatest zest, until I saw her stretch her legs out and sink backwards on the bed sobbing violently, while with quick hurried movements of her buttocks she responded to every thrust I made in her inflamed interior. These violent motions only lasted a few seconds, and then I felt something wet apparently issue from her, trickle over my fingers and down her thighs. She still retained her grasp of my machine, which I felt throbbing and burning more fiercely than ever and giving me more pleasure than I had ever previously experience, though in her crisis of delight she had ceased to operate upon it. I now begged of her not to stop, but to continue her employment which afforded me so much delight. Suspecting what was indeed the case, that the sight of her charms and of the enjoyment she had undergone had stirred me up to an unwonted pitch of desire which might perhaps be attended with a happy result, she good-naturedly resumed her efforts, and every succeeding movement of her hand upon the throbbing and inflamed member evidently added intensely to the flame that consumed me. She persevered until she had produced the desired result, and I saw a drop or two of white liquid burst from the inflamed point, while at the same time a most delicious sensation pushed through the part affected and from thence seemed to thrill through my whole frame, as overcome with the exquisite delight. I fell back upon the bed, she kissing me tenderly and congratulating me on having at length attained the powers of a man; then she left me to my repose.

"After this we omitted no opportunity that was afforded us of amusing ourselves together in the same way. My ignorance on the subject, however, prevented me from thinking of carrying our enjoyment farther, and though doubtless she knew better, she allowed me to return to school without enlightening me any farther. She made me promise two things, first that I was not to indulge myself in any repetition of our pastimes until we met again, and secondly not to say anything to my schoolfellows regarding such subjects. I cannot say that I kept my promise on either point. I tried as well as I could to do so with regard to the first, but I could not help occasionally breaking through. But my curiosity was too much excited by our late proceedings not to endeavour to ascertain how some of my elder companions felt regarding such subjects. On sounding them cautiously I discovered that some of them were better informed on such affairs than I was, and from their revelations I became aware of the amount of pleasure I had lost through my want of knowledge to avail myself of it. It so happened that during the following year whenever I was at home Laura was absent, and when we did at length occasionally meet and I endeavoured to prevail on her to afford me an op-

TWO NOVELS

portunity of repeating our old amusements, she always put me off, laughing and saying that I was
grown too old for her to allow me to play these
tricks now, so that I never have been able to show
her what a change had taken place in the size of
her old acquaintance or to prove to her how much
pleasure I am sure it could now give her."

This detail produced such an exciting effect upon
both of our organs of pleasure that we were obliged
again to quench our raging fires in each other's in-
teriors. In the course of the mutual operation I
questioned him as to whether, if he had an opportunity, he would like to repeat his former amusements with Laura and even carry them further. He
said at once it would be most delightful to do so,
and nothing would give him greater pleasure. Then
referring to her close neighbourhood to us and to
her aunt's approaching departure, he said that there
would be such a capital opportunity for our all
enjoying ourselves together, if she could only be
persuaded to agree to it, that he was determined
to try whether he could not persuade her to renew
their meetings, and he even showed me a key to
the door leading into her room which he had
got made on purpose to enable him to have access
to her.

His story had somewhat enlightened me as to
Laura's ideas, and I could now understand to some
degree her not feeling so much annoyed as I had
been at Frank's arrival. I strongly suspected that
rather than be deprived of her favourite amusement,
she would not object to his again being a partici-
pator in it. I thought it better, however, not to

say anything to him at present regarding my intimacy with her until I had ascertained what her intentions really were. After mutually agreeing that we were both to endeavour to prevail on her to join in our sports, and that if one succeeded he was to do all he could for the benefit of the other, we went down to breakfast.

I had an opportunity sooner than I expected of coming to an explanation with Laura. She had told me that she could not meet me that morning at the summer house, but in the course of the forenoon she found she could get away for an hour, and she gave me the usual signal for me to repair there. When, as she was accustomed to do, she opened my trousers and uncovered her little darling and proceeded to give him his usual caress before introducing him into his nest, her quick eye at once discovered that he was not in his ordinary trim to satisfy her desires. With a flushed cheek, she looked me full in the face, and asked what was the reason of this and what I had been about to occasion such a state of things.

I was very well pleased to have such a good opportunity of coming to the point, and I at once answered that, having been deprived of the pleasure of seeing her in the morning and despairing of being able to accomplish a meeting with her that day, I had been reduced to the necessity of seeking consolation in the embraces of one whose charms put me so much in mind of her that I had almost believed it was her in reality and had been tempted to exceed the limits I had intended to have placed upon myself.

She inquired with some heat and astonishment what I meant. But she blushed scarlet when I replied that Frank and I had been rehearsing some of her lessons. She was at first rather annoyed at what I told her; but when I explained to her that I had not made Frank aware of what had passed between us until I was sure of her approbation and that his reason for confiding in me was the hope of my being of use in enabling him to obtain the bliss he so much coveted—of again regaling himself in her charms—she was quite appeased.

I had little difficulty in discerning that she was highly delighted with the glowing description I gave of his youthful charms and especially of the size and prowess of her old acquaintance. I dwelt on this and on the necessity there was of taking him into our confidence, and even making him a partner in our amusements, unless we were to give them up entirely, for there could be no doubt if we went on that he would soon discover the footing we were on. Although I could not get her to say that she would consent to this, I was tolerably well satisfied she would make no great opposition. I therefore ceased to urge the point, telling her that she must leave it to me to arrange matters with Frank, if I found it was necessary, and that I would take care not to commit her more than was absolutely requisite.

We had continued to caress each other during this conversation and her charms producing their usual effect upon me I was soon able to point out to her the flourishing condition of her favorite.

I exerted myself notwithstanding my previous night's work to show her that it had not quite exhausted me; and at length she left me quite reconciled by the result of three vigorous encounters.

When Frank came to me that night he was somewhat surprised at the state of my rather enervated champion, which he with great glee contrasted with the vigorous condition of his own. But he was still more surprised when I frankly confessed that I could not attempt to cope with him on that occasion, and explained the cause from which the deficiency arose. He was greatly delighted to learn the footing on which I stood with Laura, and at once concluded that she would not be able to resist the temptation of adding to her enjoyment by making him participate in it. I quite agreed with him, but at the same time I told him the objection she had made and that it would probably be necessary to devise some plan by which at least the appearance of her not voluntarily complying with his desires might be kept up.

After some deliberation on this subject, occasionally interrupted by a renewal of our previous evening's amusements, in which, however, I generally allowed my young friend to take the more active share, we arranged our plan which was carried into effect in this manner.

Laura was now afraid to venture to the summer house every morning, so we had few opportunities of meeting. But ascertaining that her mother and her aunt were going two days afterwards to pay a visit at a distance, which would occupy them the whole forenoon, I arranged with her that if she were left alone, she should come to my room where I would be waiting for her. I then arranged with Frank that at breakfast he should say he was going to take a ride to call upon a companion in the neighbourhood, but that instead of doing so he should conceal himself in a closet in my room and upon my giving a certain signal he should make a noise which would lead to his discovery without it appearing that I knew he was there.

Everything happened as I anticipated. As soon as the carriage drove off with her mother, Laura came to my room, where I was awaiting her. Saying that it seemed an age since I had had the opportunity of fully enjoying the sight and touch of all her charms, I at once stripped myself quite naked and proceeded to perform the same operation upon her. As she enjoyed this as much as I did, she made no objection whatever, and even assisted in getting rid of her clothes as fast as possible. I placed her in several different postures, in order to allow the delighted boy to enjoy the voluptuous sensations I was sure her charms would produce upon him, and then proceeded to the final enjoyment. When this had been completed to our mutual satisfaction, I again displayed all her attractions, and when by kisses and caresses and lascivious touches I had again roused her desires for a repetition of the encounter, I made the agreed-on signal to Frank. He immediately responded by pushing down some article of furniture. Laura started up, exclaiming, "Good heavens, what is that? Can anyone be there?"

I jumped out of the bed and seized a pistol

which was lying on the dressing table and opened the door saying I would take good care to silence any intruder so that he should never be able to tell upon us. On opening the door and disclosing Frank, I exclaimed, "So it is you, Master Peeping Tom. Well, it is lucky it is only you, for anyone else would have had a good chance of having a bullet through his head. But I shall deal somewhat differently with you. Don't suppose, however, you are to get off unpunished for thus stealing in upon us. I see there is a good rod here, and you shall have a sound flogging for your impertinence and curiosity. So strip instantly and remember the longer you are about it the more severe your punishment will be."

Frank appeared nothing loth to submit to the proposed infliction and with my assistance was soon as naked as we were.

All this time I watched Laura closely to observe how she was affected by our proceedings. At first she had been dreadfully alarmed, but on finding it was only Frank she was quite aware she was perfectly safe. As I proceeded to strip him, and disclosed his exquisite figure and symmetrical proportions, she evidently became much interested, and when at last I drew his shirt over his head and revealed the full contour of his body with his delicious charmer standing fully erect and exhibiting its rosy head completely developed, I could see a flash of pleasure and delight steal over her lovely features and impart still greater animation to her sparkling eyes. Convinced that I might now proceed to any extremities I said, "Now, Laura, you

must assist me to punish this young rogue properly.''

I then gave her the rod, and sitting down on
the side of the bed, I placed him across my knees
and turned up his beautiful posteriors to her. She
instantly entered into the sport and gave him two
or three cuts with the birch which, though not
very severe, were quite sufficient to give him an excuse for tossing his legs about and exhibiting all
his charms in the most voluptuous manner possible, in which I gave him every assistance in my
power. After this playful enjoyment had been continued for some time, I said to Laura that she was
too gentle with him and did not punish him half
so severely as he deserved, and proposed that she
should change places with me and let me take the
rod. She laughingly assented and asked me in what
position she was to hold him for me. I told her
the best plan would be to do as they flogged the
boys at school, and I would show her how it was
done. Making her lean forward upon the bed, I
placed him behind her, and putting his arms over
her shoulders, I made her catch hold of his hands,
telling her to hold them fast. She did as I directed,
while I applied a few lashes to his plump, handsome posteriors which, as I expected, made him
cling closely to Laura, bringing his instrument into
direct contact with her buttocks, against which it
beat furiously, as if eager to effect an entrance
somewhere.

I said, "Ah, I see you have got a very unruly
little gentleman there, I must try if we can't hold
him fast also." And at the same time I inserted it

beween her thighs and again inflicted a few blows.

The near approach of his furious weapon to the seat of pleasure caused him to make fierce efforts to endeavour to penetrate it, and I could no longer resist the imploring glances he cast upon me, expressive of his urgent desire that I should enable him to complete his enjoyment. So making Laura rest her belly on the bed and stretch her legs as far asunder as possible so as to afford him a fair entrance from behind, I loosened her hold of his arms so far as to enable him to stoop down sufficiently low, and then taking hold of his flaming weapon I guided it into the heaven which I felt was burning with desire and eager to receive it. Laura at once accommodated herself to all his proceedings and finding that her hold of his hands rather obstructed his progress, she loosened it, and they were soon transferred to her splendid swelling globes, and then, as he became more and more excited in the hot struggle, were firmly clasped round her waist so as to bring their bodies into the closest possible contact. Animated by the delicious scene before my eyes the fiery impatience of my excited organ of pleasure could no longer be restrained. I threw myself on the lovely boy and almost at the first thrust was plunged up to the hilt in the delicious buttocks which he thus so temptingly exposed to my eager assault.

Once engulphed I had nothing to do but to keep my place and leave to the energetic struggles of the other two combatants the task of bringing the warfare to a successful termination.

After a hard fight, during which the utmost

endeavours of both parties seemed to be to try which should be vanquished soonest, it terminated in a drawn battle.

And as I contributed at the same time my share of the spoil, poor Frank's beautiful little balls of delight were quite inundated both before and behind with the stream which flowed from himself and me and which mingled with the first tribute his manly prowess had drawn down from woman and poured in torrents along his thighs. The dear boy was so overcome with the delight that I thought at first he must have fainted, but I soon discovered it was only the swoon of pleasure. Raising him up in my arms, as soon as I could disengage my unruly member from the pleasant quarters it still clung too, I laid him on the bed by the side of Laura who was not in much better condition and stood equally in need of my assistance.

It is wonderful, however, how soon one recovers from such exhaustion, and in a few minutes they were both as lively as ever and were actively engaged in the mutual contemplation of each other's exquisite charms. This pleasant proceeding was enlivened by an animated discussion regarding the alteration and improvement which each of them discovered the other's beauties had undergone since they had last been submitted to their mutual inspection, and it cannot be doubted that Laura was greatly delighted to witness the change in size of the pretty little champion to which she had given the first lesson. All this, of course, produced the usual effect upon us, and Frank seeing that I was quite ready to renew the combat proposed to resign Laura to me. I fancied, however, that they would like a repetition of their previous engagement, and he was evidently perfectly able to renew it, for, indeed, the wanton boy had been so wound up by the preliminary scene that his former encounter had produced hardly any relaxing effect upon his lovely weapon. I therefore drew him upon the not unwilling Laura, and again guiding the fiery courser into the lists of pleasure, had the satisfaction of seeing them once more commence the amorous encounter, which proceeded to the ordinary happy result, evidently to the great delight of both parties.

Frank, revelling in the blissful conjunction of every part of their naked bodies, clasped Laura round the neck and imprinted burning kisses upon her lovely lips, while his rampant steed plunged violently backwards and forwards in the abyss of pleasure and his charming buttocks bounded and quivered with the excess of wanton delight. Greatly interested in watching the delightful encounter, I endeavoured to promote their enjoyment by tickling and playing with them in the most sensitive places, till their excitement reached its height and they both sunk down in the swoon of pleasure.

Laura had no sooner recovered a little from the effects of this engagement, than Frank insisted on seeing me perform the same pleasant operation in which he had just been engaged. Nothing loth, I immediately humoured his fancy, getting upon Laura, who was still lying on her back in the bed. The lascivious and not yet exhausted boy had no sooner got us fairly placed and my weapon in-

TWO NOVELS

serted in Laura's sheath and set to work, than I
felt him separate our legs so as to enable him to
kneel down between them behind us. Having established his position satisfactorily, he instantly
plunged his still rampant champion into my rear,
producing in me the most rapturous sensations,
which soon caused me in conjunction with Laura
to die away in bliss before he was ready to join
our sacrifice.

Finding that he was determined to complete his
third pleasing operation, I proposed that he should
change his position and take up my place in
Laura's palace of pleasure and allow me again to
stimulate him in the rear, and assist him to attain
his object. He highly approved of this proposal,
and immediately took up his position in Laura's
arms, while, getting behind him and inserting my
weapon in his delicious sheath, I proceeded to render
him the same agreeable service he had just done me.
This speedily had the desired effect, and a delicious
emission from all the three parties brought our
undertaking to a most successful and satisfactory
conclusion.

By this time, Laura for once had had enough to
satisfy her, and we separated, sadly grudging the
loss of the two days which were still to pass before
the departure of her aunt would admit of a renewal of our joys in security. We faithfully proposed on our part that we should be abstinent in
the meantime with the view of being the better
able to enjoy ourselves thoroughly when the happy
time for our all again meeting together should ar-
rive. Upon the whole, with the assistance of an

occasional solace from her in the summer house, when an opportunity afforded, we kept our promise tolerably well, though as Frank would insist on coming to my bed, and we could neither of us refrain from indulging in a sight of each other's charms, it was sometimes a hard struggle to restrain our desires.

At length Miss Middleton's departure enabled us to give free course to all our wanton inclinations, and night after night my room was the scene of a repetition of the most exquisite and voluptuous enjoyments it is possible to conceive. When our exhausted frames could no longer furnish us with the means of indulging in the performance of our soul-stirring rites, we were never tired of gazing on and caressing the delicious forms which were constantly exhibited without reserve for the delectation and amusement of one another, for we all seemed to feel that our own delight was heightened by aiding to promote the happiness of the others. We had no secrets from Laura; in fact, she had witnessed with delight the pleasures which Frank and I mutually conferred upon each other. On one occasion when she was disqualified from joining in our amusements, she watched Frank and me stripping and enjoying by ourselves the pleasures she was unable to participate in.

The evident delight they afforded us affected her so greatly that she declared she must try the effect of the same operation upon herself. Accordingly, the next night she insisted upon us both operating on her at the same time. Frank offered to me the choice of routes. But as I was aware that he had often contemplated with great pleasure the idea of opening up the new way, which he thought would be peculiarly well suited to his yet somewhat undeveloped proportions, I at once gave him the precedence. I told him that, as I had already had one victory over a maiden citadel, it was only fair that he should enjoy the next and that it was better he should do so, as in all probability he would obtain it with less suffering to the conquered fair one than if my larger battering ram were at first introduced. Laura quite approved of this arrangement. Having all stripped quite naked, I laid myself down in the bed at full length and then drew her upon me, making her place herself so as to bring her cavity just over the stiff pole which was standing up ready to enter it. She herself inserted and adjusted it in the most satisfactory manner. When she was quite impaled upon me and firmly fastened by the wedge being fairly driven home in her, Frank got between her legs on his knees, and with lance in hand, proceeded to insert it in her hinder cavity. Being, however, his first attempt at storming a maiden fortress, he was not very expert at it, and the coveted way proving very narrow and confined, it was not without some difficulty he effected his object. The obstacles, however, only increased the ardour of his desires and, with the assistance of a little cold cream, they were at length happily surmounted, and his weapon forced its way into the interior of the citadel. During this time I endeavoured to keep as quiet as possible, and as Frank's efforts occasioned her some pain, Laura also remained nearly motionless, only exerting herself a little occasionally to humour his movements and assist him in effecting an entrance. As soon, however, as I found from his exclamation of delight that his weapon had overcome all resistance and was as fully imbedded in the lascivious, fleshy sheath as mine was, I began at first gently and quietly, and then more rapidly and vigorously, to join in the combat, heaving my buttocks up and down and urging the lusty pole backwards and forwards in its delicious quarters, only pausing now and then to receive and return the burning kisses which Laura, now rendered quite frantic with the double enjoyment stimulating her both before and behind, showered upon me. I soon found that any further efforts on my part were quite unnecessary. Maddened by the novel excitement, Laura heaved and thrust alternately, displacing and replacing the sturdy instruments above and below, and declaring she really knew not which of them afforded her the greatest delight. I, therefore, confined myself to favouring her movements so as to give them the greatest possible effect, till at last with her eyes flashing fire and her whole body panting and heaving with the excess of her emotion, she almost shouted out, "Oh, heavens, this is too much!" Her grasp round me slackened, and she sunk entranced on my bosom, while Frank and I responded to her call, and a few frantic heaves on both our parts served to cause our rivers of delight to flow into her where, mingling with her own flood, they somewhat served to calm our overexcited senses.

It was some time before Laura came to herself,

but when she did she was delighted to find that we still retained our respective positions within her. On my inquiring whether they felt disposed for a renewal of the combat in a similar manner, they both declared with the most impassioned caresses that nothing would give them greater delight.

Telling Frank that as the entrance to both fortresses was now well lubricated, we might venture to carry on the warfare more boldly without the risk of doing any damage. I desired him to keep time with me and thrust his weapon as far in and out as he could at each heave, first alternately with me and then on a given signal both together.

At the same time I advised Laura to remain quiet and try what would be the effect of our efforts. The result far surpassed her expectations. When, after heaving alternately for some little time, I gave Frank the signal and we made a simultaneous thrust together, burying both our weapons as far as they would go within the soft yielding flesh, she exclaimed, "Oh, this is exquisite, it could not possibly be more heavenly." We continued this mode of action for some time, alternately changing from one variety to another, while she responded merely by twisting and wriggling her buttocks, and in turn compressing and squeezing the darling object before or behind. which for the moment affected her senses the more powerfully. Gradually, however, she became too much animated to adhere to any settled plan, and she could not refrain from meeting and returning our lusty efforts to promote her enjoyment. This only animated us to fresh exertions in which we were so successful that we were soon rewarded by as over-powering an overflow of bliss as before.

As soon as it was over, she insisted on laying us both out at full length on the bed quite naked, bringing our organs of pleasure so close together that she could caress them at the same time, and placing herself upon us so that her mouth came in contact with them. In this position she remained for a long time—kissing, caressing, and sucking the instruments of delight and thanking us in the warmest manner for the excessive joy we had given her until her luscious caresses, exciting us almost to madness, forced us again to allay the irritation produced on our burning weapons by again bring-ing them into her delightful sheaths.

In such exquisite amusements a few weeks passed rapidly away without any interruption to our joys, when we were startled by learning from Laura that there was a derangement of the usual symptoms which she feared indicated pregnancy. This greatly alarmed us, for trusting to our youth we had had no fear on this subject. I lost no time in consulting an eminent London surgeon, but his reply was that the symptoms were usual in cases of pregnancy, but that they were not infallible signs of it, as they sometimes occurred from other causes. It was, however, obvious that some arrangement must be made to provide for the occurrence of the possible event. I, of course, told Laura that if it should turn out as she feared, we must make up our minds to run off together and, getting up a story of her having been previously privately mar-ried, keep out of the way until the noise of the affair blew over. This plan, however, did not meet her approbation. She said that whatever might really have been the case, everyone would at once say from the difference in our ages that she must have seduced me and that she would never be able to show her face again in society, and that moreover she could not think of inflicting such a penalty on me as to saddle me for life with a wife older than myself, when she had been as much to blame in the matter as I had.

After a great deal of consideration I ventured to hint whether her best plan would not be to accept Sir Charles Tracy, marry him at once, and get the ceremony over without delay, so that if a child did come, there might be at least the lapse of six months to admit of the possibility of his being the father.

I must here explain that Sir Charles had been an almost constant resident at the Hall ever since my arrival, and was evidently looked upon by the family as a suitor. He was a young man of about twenty-seven, of large fortune, tall, handsome, and well made, not particularly clever, but almost the best-tempered and most good-natured person I ever met. His object in remaining so long was quite obvious. Although she would never admit it, I had all along fancied that Laura liked him; but since I had become so intimate with her, she certainly had shown more coldness towards him than she did on my first arrival.

At first, Laura said this plan would never do. But, as we could devise nothing else, on my pressing her a little on the subject she admitted that before I came she had made up her mind to accept him if he proposed, but that she was afraid to do so now for two reasons: first, she feared he might discover on his first attack that someone had had access before him to the sanctuary of love, and secondly, from the dread that in the event of a child coming before the usual time he might denounce her and turn her adrift.

I considered a little, and then asked her whether if these difficulties could be got over she would still be disposed to marry him.

She said it was no use thinking of it, but that if it were not for the objections she had mentioned, she certainly would, as she thought she could live happily with him.

I then told her that as to the first objection she might set her mind perfectly at ease, for from what I had already seen of Sir Charles, his instrument I knew was so much larger than anything that had found its way into her and he would find so much difficulty in getting it in for the first time that he would never suspect any intruder had been before him, and that if, as she easily might, she insisted in the operation being performed in the dark, I could supply her with a contrivance by which a little red liquid might be applied so as to produce the natural appearance of an effusion of blood. Then as to the second objection, I told her I thought there would be little fear of his making any complaint at least in public on the subject, if she had the power to hold out to him that she could bring forward a matter which it would be equally unpleasant for him to have disclosed.

She said that in such a case the matter might perhaps be arranged, but she could not imagine how she was to obtain such a hold over him.

I told her I thought she might leave that to me. I then explained to her that Sir Charles had taken a fancy to me on my arrival, and had shown me every kindness and attention, evidently wishing to be on an intimate footing with me.

The poor fellow no doubt was in an awkward predicament. Inflamed by the constant sight of the charms of Laura, of whom he was greatly enamoured, he was afraid to console himself in the arms of any of the women in the neighbourhood for fear his infidelity might come to her knowledge, and unable wholly to restrain his desire to give vent in some manner to his pent-up passions, he had made some overtures to me of which I clearly understood the meaning, though with Laura, Betsy, and Frank on my hands, I had quite enough to do in that way, and consequently I had pretended not to understand his intentions. I now suggested to Laura that by complying with his wishes I might get him to come to my room where she and Frank would have an opportunity of seeing us enjoy each other, so that if at any future period he should accuse her of infidelity prior to her marriage, she might retort upon him.

Laura was quite satisfied that, if this could be accomplished, she would be perfectly safe; as with his good temper she said she had little doubt, even in case of the worst we dreaded occurring, she would be able to persuade him that it would be for the interests of both that he should keep quiet, seeing she had such a hold over him. She now admitted that she really was fond of him, though her curiosity and my boldness had lately enabled me to gain the advantage over him, and I easily drew from her that she did not like him the less for the report I had made of his evident ability to perform satisfactorily in the battles of Venus. I therefore told her that, though I was afraid that the performance of the instrument that would probably afford the greatest pleasure to her might prove to be martyrdom to me, I was prepared to undergo it for her sake, and we signed and sealed the agreements in our usual happy way.

As I have always found that where a thing is once determined on it is better to lose no time in carrying it into execution, I set to work immediately. I dressed for dinner that day sooner than usual, and about half an hour before the ordinary dinner hour, I made my way to Sir Charles' room, taking with me an amorous work he had lent me and making a pretext of wishing to borrow another. When he found who it was that knocked at the door he asked me to come in, saying that he wanted to see me as he had that day received a packet from town with some things he had ordered down for me. He then told his servant to lay out some things for him, and that he would not be required further. As soon as the servant had left the room, he took from a drawer a large parcel, and selecting a packet of drawings, told me to sit down and amuse myself with them while he finished dressing.

This was coming to the point even sooner than

I had anticipated, but as it was just the opening I wanted, I sat down and began to examine the drawings which consisted of a most beautifully executed series of voluptuous designs. When he had dressed himself, all except his coat and waistcoat (and he was a very few minutes about it), he came and leaned over me, looking at the drawings and making observations upon them. After we had gone over them, he said there were some more which he liked still better and he hoped I would be equally well pleased with them. He went to the drawer for them, while I rose up to lay aside those we had been looking at. He selected two packets, and then coming back to the easy chair in which I had been sitting, he sat down, and wished to draw me on his knee.

This, however, I did not allow, but I sat down on the arm of the chair allowing him to put his arm round my waist. He exhibited some more illustrations of luscious scenes, many of which were new to me, and I did not attempt to conceal the effect which was produced upon me, while I told him, which was the case, that I had never seen anything of the kind more beautifully designed and executed. I could see that he was watching the impression made not only on my face but also on another part of my person, which had now become somewhat prominent. He seemed satisfied with this, and then opened the other packet, which was a series of drawings executed by a first-rate artist in the most admirable style delineating the seduction of a beautiful young boy of about fifteen by another handsome youth a few years older.

Every scene in the progress was illustrated by an appropriate and admirably drawn portrait of the two characters, commencing with taking him on his knee and impressing the first amorous kiss; the laying of his hand upon the organ of pleasure; the maiden bashfulness of first feeling the naked weapon grasped by a strange hand; the first starting out of the beautiful object on the trousers being unloosened; the full development of all its beauties on their being removed; the drawing his bridle over the fiery little head of the charger; the playing with the beautiful little appendices; the opening the thighs to get a glimpse of the seat of pleasure behind; the turning him round to obtain a full view of the exquisite hindquarters; the first exposure to his gaze of the second actor in the scene of pleasure; the making him caress and play with it; the complete exposure of all their naked charms as their shirts are drawn over their heads; the close embrace as they strain each other in their arms; the turning him round to present the altar for the sacrifice; the entrance; the combat; the extasy; the offering the recompensing pleasure; the introducing the virgin weapon for the first time; the ardour of the first enjoyment; the first tribute and the mutual embrace of thanks as they kissed and caressed each other's organs of pleasure after the work happily was accomplished. All these were depicted with a beauty and a truth to nature that forcibly reminded me of my own sweet experience of similar enjoyment on my first initiation in the secrets of pleasure. As I gazed with admiration upon them, he could not help observing how much

I was interested, and was no doubt encouraged to think, as I intended he should be, that there would be little objection on my part to his proceeding to enact a similar scene. His hand gradually slipped down over my stiffly distended weapon. I made a little faint resistance, but gradually allowed him, without much difficulty, to handle and feel it, to unloosen my trousers and make it appear on the stage. He had no sooner got possession of it, than he loaded it with kisses and caresses, declaring that he had never seen anything to surpass it in beauty. He had not much more difficulty in loosening my braces and completely removing my trousers so as to give him a full opportunity of seeing and handling my naked person.

I affected to be so much engrossed with the pictures as not to observe that he had not only done this, but had also drawn down his own trousers and raised up his shirt displaying his magnificent weapon, until taking my hand he tried to make me grasp—for my fingers could not meet round it—by far the most splendid and largest champion I had ever met with, one which, indeed, I have never seen surpassed. He seemed much amused by my surprised exclamation, "Oh, goodness, what a monster," and, laughing, asked if I had never seen one so large before. But on my expressing my wonder that he should ever get it into a woman at all he seemed to be a little apprehensive that I might be too much frightened to allow it to enter where he wished it should go, and he tried to persuade me that after all there was not so very great a difference between it and mine.

In truth I had begun to be somewhat terrified on the subject and to wish at least to delay the operation, if it must be undergone, until it could be effected in a place where the object desired could be secured. I knew that in a few minutes the dinner bell would ring, and I therefore determined to temporize as long as possible and escape on the present occasion by holding out hopes of his attaining his object on a more favourable opportunity.

But I found that it was easier to make the resolution than to keep it. His evident passion for me and the means he adopted to excite me to an ardour equal to his own—keeping up a titillatory friction over the most sensitive points of my body—soon produced their effect, and in spite of my resolution, I could not make any effort to oppose him. Having drawn me on his knees, he raised me up, and opening my buttocks and holding apart the lips of the orifice, he presented the enormous head of his charger and tried to gain admittance. He seemed to be aware that there must be considerable difficulty, and he not only anointed the parts with cold-cream, but he also refrained from attempting to force it in by any violent exertion on his part, apparently wishing that the junction should be brought about in a manner that would run less risk of occasioning me pain by my pressing gently down upon it myself. This he urgently begged me to do, and I could not withhold feeling sensible of this attention to my feelings on his part. I thought it would be hardly fair of me not to show that I was so by at least endeavouring, as far as I could, to aid in accomplishing his wishes. I therefore pressed down upon the impaling stroke with as much force as I could venture to exert, and with great difficulty and some pain did get the head fairly within the entrance. Having attained this, I desisted from my efforts for a moment and was pleased to find that the pain ceased entirely. As for him, he was perfectly enchanted and loaded me with kisses and caresses. Just then the bell announced that dinner would be on the table in five minutes. Although I had previously been anxiously expecting this announcement, I must confess I felt sorry when it did come, for I had now got so interested and excited in our proceedings that I would willingly have contributed by every means in my power, even at any sacrifice of pain, to bring the enterprise to a successful termination. But there seemed no help for it, and I turned my head round to him and said that I was afraid we must go downstairs. He caught me round the neck, pressed my lips passionately to his, and entreated me to have patience with him for a few moments; he said he would not attempt to do anything that would give me more pain, but that he was then enjoying the most transcendent pleasure from the kind assistance I had already afforded him in getting his instrument so far imbedded in the abode of bliss, and if I would only allow him to remain where he was for a few seconds longer, he would be overwhelmed with the excess of his joy and would never cease to be grateful to me for having thus contributed to it. I could not resist his appeal, seeing clearly from his excited and flashing eyes that the tempest was nearly at its height, and on the eve of bursting forth with all the fury of a torrent.

He did not attempt to force his way further in, but supporting me with his arms he wriggled and twisted his buttocks making his weapon move about within me in the most surprising and delicious manner. Wishing to gratify and assist him as far as I could, I put one hand behind and grasping as well as I could the lower part of the splendid pillar, I rubbed and squeezed it, endeavouring to increase the excitement and promote his object; then passing the other hand between my thighs, I tickled and played with the massy round globes I found just beneath my own and which instead of hanging down, pendant as at first, were now closely drawn up in their wondrous purse. He kissed me again fervently and was in the act of thanking me for my kindness in thus increasing his pleasure, when he suddenly stopped short with a passionate exclamation of a single "Oh!" My hand, which grasped his splendid weapon, was sensible of the instant rush of the fiery liquid through it, and the next moment, I felt the warm gush driven into my entrails as if it had been forced up by a pump. I continued the motion of my hand gently upon his instrument until the fit of pleasure was entirely over. Then, with some difficulty disengaging myself from the link that bound us together, I wiped the ruby head of the still rampant champion, and stooping down, first kissed it and then his lips as he still lay reclining in the chair and then proceeded to arrange my dress. He soon recovered himself and earnestly begged that I would come to his room that night that he might have an opportunity of thanking me and of endeavouring to repay, as far as he possibly could, the delicious treat I had afforded him. This, however, I would not promise to do, saying I was too much afraid of being seen when I could have no excuse for being in his room, but I allowed him to understand that I would try to devise some plan for another meeting.

I contrived to give Laura a hint before dinner that all was right and that she would get the details at night. She was so delighted with this that the distance and hauteur with which she had lately treated Sir Charles were greatly removed, and he on his part, animated by the scene which had just taken place and his victory, as he thought, over my virgin charms, was more lively and bolder than usual. So that by the end of the evening they were on a better and more familiar footing than they had even been before. When the ladies retired to bed, Sir Charles again urged me to go to his room. I still refused, but at last I suggested that perhaps he might come to me early the next morning, as this would be less liable to suspicion, for if anyone saw him we might go out immediately together, when it would be supposed he had only come for the purpose of calling me, while if he was not observed, he might remain for a time with me. Of course, that night I explained to Laura and Frank all that had passed, and we contrived to make two apertures in the partition wall of the closet between Frank's room and mine, from which they would have an uninterrupted view of the scene of operations.

The next morning I heard Sir Charles open my door, but I lay quiet as if still asleep. I was conscious that he fastened the door and then came round to the side of the bed where I was lying. He removed the bed-clothes, raised up my nightshirt, and remained for some minutes contemplating me. Of course, the principal object of his worship was my virile member which, as was usual at that period of my life, always held up its head proudly erect when I awoke in the morning. I heard him undress himself and get into bed, and then kneeling down by my side, after kissing and caressing my organ of pleasure, he took the point of it into his mouth and commenced sucking it and moving it backwards and forwards between his lips. I opened my eyes, as if just awakened, and beheld him kneeling beside me perfectly naked with his tremendous member standing stiff and erect. He immediately made me take off my shirt, and employed himself for a time in examining me all over and caressing all my charms. During this time I also made a more minute inspection of my acquaintance of the preceding evening, and I was even more than ever astonished at its proportions, and at how I had managed ever to get it within my narrow aperture as far as it had been.

After some little time had elapsed in these preliminaries, he said that it was his turn now to contribute to my enjoyment, and taking hold of my weapon, he was going to turn himself away from where Laura and Frank were placed. As they had both been greatly interested by the account I had given them of Sir Charles' tremendous weapon, I wished that they should have an opportunity of seeing as much as possible of its proceedings. So I got him to change his position and to place himself where they were and where they could have the gratification of observing every motion he made in the approaching encounter. He immediately placed himself as I wished, and I then, at his request, took up my position behind him, and he proceeded to introduce my weapon into the sheath of pleasure. But if I had been surprised at the largeness of one of his proportions, I was no less so at the smallness of the other, as in fact I had almost as much difficulty in getting into him as he had had with me. At length, with his assistance, I succeeded and gradually penetrated within the delightful cavity, till I was completely imbedded within it. Of course, the opposition I met with and the extreme tightness of the place, when it was once fairly overcome, only increased the pleasurable sensations I experienced after I had fairly accomplished my entrance. When he found I was completely buried within him and was beginning to proceed with the work of pleasure, he took my hand and placed it on his majestic champion, saying that if I would be good enough to operate upon it at the same time it would not only give him exquisite pleasure by being combined with the performance going on behind, but would also, by depriving it of a little of its vehement fury, make our after-proceedings more easy and agreeable to me, when, as he hoped I would allow him to do, he should again try to introduce it into the delicious aperture that had given him so much delight the previous day. I immediately acquiesced, and grasping as much of the pillar as I could manage to do with one hand, I commenced a series of movements upon it, gently rubbing it up and down and titillating the shaft as much as possible, which drew from him the warmest encomiums. In this manner, combining the movements of my hand in front with those of my excited weapon in the rear, I managed to pour my tribute into him at the same time that he sent a shower of love's balsam spouting beyond the bed far into the room.

This scene acted so powerfully on Laura that unable to restrain herself, as Frank afterwards told me, she seized hold of his hand, conveyed it to her pleasure-spot, and made him cool her raging fever in a similar manner where she stood.

Sir Charles then asked if I would allow him to endeavour to accomplish the undertaking which it had given him so much delight partially to accomplish the preceding day. I could not well make any objection, after having availed myself of his complaisance, to his now proceeding to carry out his wishes to their entire fulfilment. I therefore disposed myself so as to endeavour to stand the attacks in as favourable a position as I could, and at the same time afford my friends as good a view of the proceedings as was possible.

I placed all the pillows and cushions I could find on a heap in the centre of the bed and lay down with my belly resting on them so as to raise up my posteriors and present them to him in an attitude that would be propitious to his purpose. He thanked me, and told me to let him know if I found that he hurt me too much and he would at once stop, as he would be sorry to enjoy even such a gratification if it were to be at the expence of occasioning me any suffering. He had provided some ointment with which he lubricated the whole of his weapon, and then with his finger inserted some of it in my aperture. He then applied the point of the dart to the mark, and endeavoured to insert it. For some time it baffled his endeavours, the head slipping upwards and downwards, away from the entrance, whenever he attempted to thrust which he did very gently and carefully. I saw he was too much afraid of hurting me to be able to succeed, and getting excited myself by this time, put my hand between my thighs and taking hold of his splendid weapon I kept its head at the mouth of the aperture, and desired him to thrust a little more boldly. At the same time, trying to push back and stretch the aperture as much as possible, I met his advancing thrusts with all the firmness I could muster. This brought about the junction I desired, and again to his great delight the head of his weapon got lodged between the extended lips of the aperture. The pain, however, of this proceeding was so great that I was obliged to ask him to pause till it should abate a little, which it very soon did. Then summoning up courage, I told him to thrust again gently. This he hastened to do in the most delicate manner possible. The first few thrusts, till the upper part of the pillar got fairly

inserted within the cheeks, were even worse than
before. But as soon as this was accomplished, and
the hollow part at the junction of the pillar with
the head had passed the Rubicon, all feeling of un-
easiness vanished and was succeeded by the most
delicious sensations, as inch by inch he gradually
fought his way into my interior, the intense pleasure increasing at every thrust he gave, until the
whole of the monster was fairly established within
me, and I could feel the hair on his thighs and
belly in close contact with my buttocks, and his
delightful soft bullets beating against mine at
every motion he made. As soon as he was fully
lodged to the utmost extent within the citadel, he
stopped and inquired how I felt and expressed the
greatest satisfaction at finding my sufferings had
now been converted into pleasure. After enjoying
the voluptuous sensations of the elastic constriction
the nerves of the sheath in which it was plunged
exerted upon his throbbing weapon for some minutes, during which his hands roved over my body
in nervous agitation, he resumed his delightful exercise, and thrust after thrust of his delicious
weapon was driven into me with the most intense
enjoyment to both parties. At length, his lusty
efforts were rewarded with success, and, from the
warm gush within me, I felt that a torrent of bliss
must have issued from him, while his nervous
frame shook and quivered with blissful agitation
and enjoyment as the extasy of delight came over
him. He lay for a few minutes bathed in enjoyment, and then raising his head, thanked me most
fervently for all the bliss I had conferred on him

and expressed his hope that it had been accomplished without much suffering on my part. In answer I gently turned both him and myself on one side, too much delighted with its presence to allow his sword to escape from my scabbard, and made him look at the pillow on which my weapon had rested, and where a plenteous effusion of the balmy liquid plainly attested that I too had shared in the delights of his enjoyment. He expressed his great gratification at this, as he said the sole drawback to his enjoyment had been the fear that it had been attained at my expense. But he said that what he now saw emboldened him to make a new request, and as the difficulty had now been overcome, to ask whether I might be persuaded to allow him still to retain his present quarter and enjoy another victory. I readily agreed. I told him that the sensations produced upon me by the insertion of his weapon in so sensitive a place was so agreeable—that it was so was, indeed, very evident from the powerful manner in which it still affected mine—that he must allow it to remain quietly where it was for a time and let me enjoy the agreeable sensation of its presence there.

He said he could desire nothing better, and we lay for a considerable period thus pleasantly conjoined. During this time I purposely turned the conversation upon Laura and Frank. I began by joking him about what Laura would say if she saw us in such a situation defrauding her of her just rights. He replied that he did not know what she would say, but that he knew what she ought to say, or at least what he would say if he were to find her in a similar situation, and that was that as she could not assist in contributing to his happiness at present, she was very glad to find that he had been able to get somebody else who could.

"Then," said I, "you would not be offended, if she were to follow your example."

"No, certainly not," was his reply. "I don't mean to say that I would not rather prefer that I should have her entirely to myself, but I am so fond of her that if I found it would contribute to her happiness to enjoy herself with another, I should not make the slightest objection, provided she would only allow me to contribute to her enjoyment as much as I could." He went on to say that he was sadly afraid she would never allow him that pleasure, that he did once hope she might have been induced to accept him, but for the last few weeks, with the exception of the previous night, she had been colder than ever, and he was afraid to press her on the subject for fear of being at once rejected.

I ventured cautiously to express my opinion that he was too distrustful of his own merits, and that he stood higher in Laura's favour than he seemed to imagine.

He eagerly caught at my words, and asked on what grounds I thought so. He said he saw that from my old acquaintance with her as a boy, I was on more intimate terms with her than anyone else and more likely to understand her sentiments, and that he had often thought of speaking to me on the subject. Indeed, he said he would almost have been jealous of my influence with her had I been a few years older and had it not been that, instead of appearing to be annoyed at his attentions to her, I had rather given him every opportunity to pursue them.

As I felt he was watching me, I endeavoured to keep my countenance as well as I could, but I was aware that the blood mounting in my cheeks must to some extent betray the secret interest I took in the subject. I though the best plan was to acknowledge that from our early intimacy, and the kindness she had always shown me, I did take a great interest in her, and that it was perhaps only my being sensible that she could neither look up to nor respect one so much younger than herself that prevented this feeling from ripening into a warmer attachment, but that I was old enough to be able to wish to promote her happiness even if I could not myself be the means of doing so, and that from what I had seen of her feelings towards him, I had always thought they might be happy together, and consequently had wished him success.

He pressed me very much regarding what she thought, or might have said of him.

I told him that of course it was not a subject on which I could have ventured to speak to her seriously, that sometimes a looker-on saw more of the game than the players, and that I thought she did like him and was only restrained from showing it more by his not urging his suit so much as he perhaps might have done. We had some further conversation on the subject, and I added that I knew she was of a reserved disposition as regarded her own feelings and did not like to have them no-

ticed and commented on by strangers and that perhaps the idea of all the parade and show which he
might think necessary at the celebration of his marriage and the discussion of the matter for months
previously might annoy her, while she would probably have been more easily induced to consent had
he been a person of less rank and consequence,
when all this exhibition would have been avoided.

He said that if she had any difficulty on this
ground, nothing could be easier than to obviate it,
for as far as he was concerned it would give him the
greatest satisfaction to dispense with all formalities,
except necessary settlements which he would take
care should not occupy much time, and they might
be quietly married at their own church in the
neighbourhood without making any fuss about it;
that with the exception of his mother and sister
he had no relations he cared anything about or
whom he would wish to be present, so that Laura
could have everything her own way.

Without attempting to urge too much, I gave
him to understand that I thought he had better
come to an explanation with her as soon as possible and make her aware of his ideas on these
points. And I promised to endeavor to ascertain
her wishes as far as I could, and make him acquainted with them.

I had long felt by the unruliness of his member,
which was deeply imbedded within me, how powerful an impression the discussions of this subject
produced upon him. He very soon disregarded my
injunctions to keep quiet—the delightful intruder
would keep wandering up and down in the path

of pleasure—and before our conversation was concluded, I felt the warm injection twice spouted into
me. After this, he said he would not venture to
trespass upon my kindness any further for the present, and urged me to take his place, which, excited as I was by his performances, I was very well
disposed to do. He made every arrangement for
my entering him in the most agreeable manner, inserting the weapon himself and tickling and playing with the appendages.

When fairly entered and enjoying myself to the
utmost, I laughingly said that if he was going to
run away with Laura I could not hope for any
long continuance of our present agreeable amusement and I must try if I could persuade Frank to
allow me to enjoy with him some of the pleasant
pastimes he had been teaching me. He eagerly
caught at the idea and urged me to do so, offering
to leave with me all his books and pictures to show
to him, and telling me to let him have any of them
he liked, and at the same time begging me, if I
succeeded, to allow him to join in our amusements,
as the possession of one resembling Laura so much
would be the next thing to enjoying herself. This
was exactly what I wanted, for I felt satisfied that
after having enjoyed the brother he could never
complain of anything the sister might do. Having
then brought my enterprise to a satisfactory termination, I made him leave me, and joined Laura
and Frank.

Although they had been able to see everything,
they had not heard all that passed. Coming to my
bed, they proceeded to satisfy the burning desires

which the scene they had just witnessed had lighted up in them. While thus agreeably employed, I joked Laura about the martyrdom I had undergone for her sake and what she was to look forward to suffer when she attempted to take in the stupendous instrument whose performances she had just seen. She did not appear to be much afraid of it, and said that judging from the manner in which I had apparently enjoyed its presence within me there was not much reason for apprehension. But she eagerly asked what we had been talking about, as she had heard only so far as to make out that she was the subject of our discourse. She was quite delighted to find that the result had been so satisfactory, and it was at once resolved that, when Sir Charles pressed the matter, she would consent and that I should contrive to impress upon him the propriety of his urging the completion of the marriage with as little delay and ceremony as possible.

Frank and I made up a party to ride with them that forenoon, and we took care to let them have an opportunity for an explanation. Laura was in a gracious mood. Sir Charles acted on my advice, pressed his suit, was accepted, explained his own wish to have the marriage concluded as soon as possible, but at the same time saying that on that point as on every other he should wish to consult her feelings in every respect, and was given to understand that her sentiments coincided with his. Having obtained her consent, he spoke to her father as soon as we returned from our ride, and as the settlements he proposed were most satisfactory, it was at once arranged. And it was settled that the marriage should take place within a month.

When Sir Charles came to me the next morning, he was in extasies at the successful termination of his suit, which he asserted was in a great measure due to my good advice, and he urged me to attend him on the happy occasion. As this afforded a good excuse for my remaining at the Hall, and being on a good footing with Laura, I readily agreed. Laura having expressed a wish that they should be quiet during the few weeks she was to remain at home, it was arranged that the visits of some friends who were expected should be postponed. Her aunt, immediately on hearing of the marriage, returned to the Hall, but I made Laura give her mother a hint that, though she did not like to say so to her aunt herself, she would prefer being allowed to enjoy the privacy of an apartment by herself. Her mother thought this was quite reasonable, and another room was prepared for Miss Middleton. Frank was allowed to remain at home till after the marriage, and we thus secured another month of our delightful pastime to which we gave ourselves up without scruple or reserve. Sir Charles, though unwilling to tear himself away from the pleasure he was enjoying and anticipating, was obliged to go to town to make the necessary arrangements. I was desirous before he went to take a photographic view of him in the act of enjoying me, as I thought that in the event of Laura being obliged to have recourse to any compulsion upon him, her object would be better attained by making him aware she was in possession of such a picture than by any reference to me or explanation as to how she came to know anything on the subject. It was necessary for this purpose to bring Frank on the scene. As he was quite willing to join in the sport, having been greatly taken with what he had witnessed of Sir Charles' operations, I told the latter that by means of his pictures I had come to a good understanding with him and that he had agreed to comply with our wishes. Giving him to believe that there was a double maidenhead to be taken, I proposed that they should both be disposed of at the same time, and offered him his choice which he would prefer. He said that if it was left to him to decide he would prefer to make the attack in the rear, and we settled that he should come to me the next morning when I could get Frank to meet us.

Frank was in bed with me when Sir Charles arrived. I at once turned down the bed-clothes, stripped off his shirt and exhibited him quite naked, his fiery little dart, standing erect and unhooded, exhibiting its proportions in the most splendid manner, and I asked if he had ever seen anything more beautiful. He threw himself on the charming boy and covered every part of him with kisses, while I undressed him and reduced him to a similar state of nakedness as ourselves. As soon as this was done, I prepared Frank for the sacrifice. I was apprehensive that there would be as much difficulty in introducing the magnificent weapon into his lovely, but narrow aperture as there had been in my own case, and I endeavoured to provide against the worst as satisfactorily as I could. I knelt down on the bed and made him place himself kneeling also so as to rest his belly on my back. Sir Charles then placed himself behind him and grasped him firmly round the loins, making his splendid weapon appear between his thighs, where I saw it rubbing fiercely against Frank's less mature organ. Taking hold of it and making it move back a little, I introduced my hand between Frank's thighs, and separating the lips of the delicious aperture between his lovely buttocks, I directed the point of the throbbing monster to the proper spot. Holding it firmly in the requisite position, I told Sir Charles to press it gently forwards. This he immediately did and to my great astonishment I felt it gradually advancing and slipping into the gulph of pleasure without difficulty, till I was obliged to withdraw the grasp my hand held on it. I had hardly done so when I saw the enormous pillar entirely swallowed up, and on turning my eyes to Frank's face, I could not discover on his countenance the slightest trace of pain or suffering. Satisfied that I need have no further apprehension on his account, I turned myself a little round, so as to take my part in the play, and placing myself directly before him, so as to bring my buttocks in contact with his warm soft belly, I insinuated Frank's charming little darling into my rear. While holding me fast with one arm round the middle, he grasped my stiffly erected standard with the other hand. Thinking that the power and weight of metal of Sir Charles' performer in the rear would prevent Frank from exerting himself much in the combat, I resolved to render any great exer-

tion on his part unnecessary. For keeping time with
Sir Charles' motions, I commenced a series of
heaves by which, whenever Sir Charles' weapon
was fully driven up to the hilt in his hinder quarter, his own was as fully and as pleasantly introduced within me. This delightful operation very
soon produced such a state of extatic delirium that
he could not refrain from giving vent to the most
enthusiastic praises of our performances in such a
loud tone that I was obliged to beg him to be quiet
to prevent suspicion being aroused. The delight
was too excessive to endure long, and before Sir
Charles was ready to perform his part in the final
scene, I felt the dear boy's discharge poured into
me, as his head sank upon my back and his convulsive grasp of my throbbing instrument relaxed.
I retained him in this position for a few seconds
longer, while the fierce heaves of Sir Charles, driving his steed to and fro in the delicious field of battle, testified to the soul-stirring effect that had
been produced upon him and soon relieved his high
mettled charger of a portion of his superabundant
fluid. Then withdrawing from Frank, he laid him
down on the bed, and again renewed his caresses
which very soon reanimated the slightly drooping
head of his darling charmer.

We agreed, however, that it would be better to
allow Frank to be passive in the next encounter,
and accordingly I took the centre position, and
entering Frank's delicious rear, I exposed my own
to be breached by the enormous battering ram of
Sir Charles. The assault, however, was not nearly
so terrible, and with a little care I now contrived to

take it all in, and speedily enjoyed the felicity of feeling its throbbing pulsation beating within me over the whole extent of the cavity which it so completely filled up. Frank's charming receptacle for my own heaving instrument was of that pleasing elasticity that I should not have discovered it had ever once been invaded by a larger weapon than my own, and the voluptuous sensations it produced upon my burning member as, excited to the highest pitch and swollen to the utmost extension, the fiery dart was plunged in and out of the burning furnace, were most exquisite. I felt, too, the full effect which Frank had already experienced of the greatly increased pleasure during the amorous encounter which resulted from the pressure in the interior of so large an instrument as that of Sir Charles'. And much as I had enjoyed my former encounters with them both seperately, most assuredly this one, in which they both combined their utmost efforts to produce the most lascivious sensations it is possible to conceive, far surpassed everything that had taken place previously.

Another scene of delicious toying succeeded. The darling objects which had already given us so much delight were again investigated and admired, and each new proof of the bliss they were capable of conferring upon us only made us more eager to offer up our worship to them. Another delicious combat succeeded. Sir Charles this time took the combat-position, and I again received his member within me. But my concern being now well saturated with the blissful libations that had been already poured into it, the monster slipped into me this time with very little difficulty. Frank, on the other hand, was delighted as well as surprised to discover that he had no easy task to force his way into the agreeable fortress he was about to storm in Sir Charles' rear. But the difficulty only enhanced the pleasure when the breach was fairly made, and the invader revelled in full and undisputed possession of the interior works. And if I might judge from the exclamations of delight, they both enjoyed themselves to their hearts' content when they had once gained admission to their respective destinations. So much so that after they had run one course they gave no signs of wishing to change their positions. I put my hand behind to ascertain the state of matters, and found both the heroes still in such an excited condition that I said if they were disposed to break another lance in the same lists I was quite willing to keep my place, provided Sir Charles would take my charger in hand and lead him on to participate in the pleasing conflict. This proposal was highly approved of and at once carried into effect, to the entire satisfaction of all parties. After this I made Sir Charles leave us, not wishing that we should be entirely worked out as I was quite aware poor Laura would be in a sad state if she found that we were unable to do anything in the way of appeasing her longings after the excitement she must have undergone while witnessing our voluptuous proceedings.

As soon as he was gone, Laura made her appearance and scolded us heartily for having wasted so much of our precious strength and enjoyed ourselves so completely without her. But as we each contrived to give her pretty satisfactory proof that we had not spent all our treasures, we soon put her in a good humour again; especially as Sir Charles was to leave on the next day, when she would have us all to herself again.

In the course of the day, I easily persuaded Sir Charles to allow me to take likenesses of us all three in the various attitudes of enjoying each other, one of which I took care should be sealed up and deposited where Laura would have it at command in the event of her finding it necessary to have recourse to it, even if I should not be at hand at the time. As Sir Charles was obliged after this to be almost constantly absent, we gave up to him the few nights he occasionally spent at the Hall, and the remainder were passed with Laura in a constant series of repetitions of delightful sports which, however agreeable to the actors, would involve a tiresome repetition were I to detail them.

The only variety was Frank's adventure with Betsy. Having been once accustomed to indulge his passions, he regretted sadly that the enjoyment would continue only for so short a period, as Laura and her Charles were to go abroad immediately on their marriage, and he began to look about him for some object to console him in her absence. He soon fixed upon Betsy, but he found it more difficult to obtain her consent than he had expected. When I joked her on the subject, she admitted that she liked the boy, but said she was afraid he was too young to give her much pleasure, while there was a great risk that he might talk of it and get her into a scrape. Finding that Frank was very desirous to have her, I agreed to promote his wishes. I had endeavoured to conceal as much as possible from Betsy my intercourse with Laura, but she was too quick not to have discovered that there existed a good understanding between us, though I still pretended that although we were sometimes in the habit of amusing ourselves together after her old fashion she had not yet granted me the last favour. I now told her that Laura had discovered my intercourse with her, and that previous to her own marriage she wished to see us perform the conjugal rites that she might know how to conduct herself when it came to be her turn, and that I had therefore arranged, as Frank was to be out early the next morning, Laura was to come to my room where I had promised that Betsy and I should comply with her wishes. Frank got one of his sister's caps which concealed his hair, and a nightshirt which closed in front over his breast, and it was hardly possible for anyone to tell that it was not Laura herself. Indeed, the disguise was so complete that the next time Sir Charles came to enjoy himself with us, I made Frank dress up in the same manner and pretend to be asleep in bed with me, and it was only when I could not restrain a burst of laughter at his consternation that Sir Charles discovered the trick we had played him. Nor do I think he was perfectly satisfied until the removal of Frank's shirt showed standing proof that it did not cover a woman's form.

Betsy's discovery was made in a different manner. When she came, Frank kept under the bed-clothes until I had stripped her, and getting into bed with her performed the hymenial rites in due order. When we had finished, I slipped off her on the other side of the bed from Frank, leaving her lying on her back all exposed to his observation. He commenced a survey of every part of her, joking her on the beauties he discovered and on the manner in which she had enjoyed the operation that had just been performed, and wondering whether it would give her as much satisfaction. Gradually he began to embrace her, and at last got upon her, asking me if that was the way Sir Charles would do it to her.

"Yes that is it," said I, as he got between her thighs and placed himself in the position in which I had lately been, "only he would not have this stupid night dress about him, and he will have something stiff between his legs to put into that pretty little hole you see before you, now try what you can do to imitate him."

While Frank clasped her in his arms and pressed his mouth to hers, I raised his shirt, and pointing his weapon at the mark, he thrust himself forward, and it slipped into her in an instant. Betsy's consternation was extreme as she felt the warm flesh within her. She had on many occasions tried the effect of Laura's substitute, but her experience of the real article had been quite enough to satisfy her that this was something of a different description, and she exclaimed, "Goodness gracious Miss Laura, what is the meaning of this?"

Frank replied, tearing off his cap and exhibiting

his short curls instead of Laura's flowing ringlets, "Well, I am glad I have got something to prove I am not a girl, for I was beginning to be afraid that the change of dress had effected a complete transformation."

It was too late for any objection now. Nor did Betsy appear at all disposed to make any. On the contrary, the lascivious boy's motions were so lively and so well directed and his capacity for conferring pleasure so much greater than she had expected that she at once yielded herself up to the enjoyment, and joined in his amorous transports with hearty good will. And when he had given and drawn from her the first proof of their mutual satisfaction with each other and the young rogue still retained his position and proceeded to give her a second dose of his prolific balm, she was quite transported with delight and exerted herself with so much vigor and set to second his endeavours that they very soon sank exhausted in each other's arms enjoying to the utmost the second proof of the completion of their mutual overwhelming bliss.

But these hours of happiness were too delightful to last long. The day appointed for the marriage came upon us before we could believe it possible. Though sorely against my will I thought it right to suggest to Laura whether it would not be prudent that she should pass the last night of her presumed virgin state without having her inmost recesses explored for fear of any traces being left. But though she at first agreed that this precaution would be advisable, she could not make up

her mind to put it in practice. To our surprise and
joy she came to us as usual as soon as she was left
alone for the night. Unwilling to run the risk of
her appearing fatigued and exhausted in the morning, we resolved to concentrate our forces upon her
and take our farewell that night. Time after time
we kept up the amorous combat, sometimes in suc-
cession and sometimes combining our forces for a
joint attack both in front and rear, almost without intermission until we were fairly exhausted;
and it was only when after repeated engagements
even her fond caresses failed to revive our enervated
champions that, taking an affectionate farewell,
she retired to her own apartment. The exercise so
far from injuring seemed to have a beneficial effect
on her charms, and never had she looked more
lovely than she appeared the next morning when
she was transferred to the arms of the enraptured
Sir Charles.

Most fortunately everything turned out eventu-
ally even more agreeably than we had ventured to
hope. A few days afterwards I had the gratification of hearing from Laura that she had satisfactorily put in operation the device I had suggested,
which, combined with the difficulty Sir Charles
experienced from his great size in obtaining an entrance and the pain she pretended to experienced
when he forced his way within her supposed virgin
sanctuary, completely prevented any suspicion on
his part. And loving her as I did, I was pleased
with her frank avowal that not only his general
conduct and kindness left her nothing to wish for,
but that in her nuptial intercourse with him she

derived if possible even greater pleasure than she enjoyed with us. The symptoms which had alarmed us passed off without producing the dreaded consequence, and it was not till some weeks after the usual time had elapsed that she presented the delighted Sir Charles with a son who was soon followed by numerous successors.

Frank before long joined the army, and in the arms of others soon found consolation, though he never forgot the charms of his first instructress. When Laura and I met again, we could not refrain from renewing our old delights and comparing the changes which had taken place in each other's charms, but with the exception of one single occasion, I believe I am the only one she ever allowed to participate with her husband in the pleasures she was so well calculated to confer.

After the marriage I got alarmed about Betsy, and regretted that I had allowed her to know so much as she did. The only remedy I could devise was to persuade her to go to a distant country where she would have no temptation to speak on the subject. On sounding her, I found that, trusting to the influence she thought she had obtained over Frank and me, she was not disposed to be removed from us. I therefore had recourse to John and found him not only much more intelligent but also more sensible than his mistress. I had not much difficulty in convincing him that if he had the means of settling in Australia he was much more likely to prosper there than by continuing in service in this country.

As a further inducement, and a reason why I

took an interest in them, I told him I had discovered that Frank had taken a fancy for Betsy and that, though there was no reason to suppose anything had occurred, it would be better they should be separated. He was quite of the same opinion, and as the consequences of the operations of some one of us upon Betsy threatened in a short time to become apparent, he made it a condition of their marriage that she should emigrate with him. As I had a strong suspicion that I had at least dug out the foundation, if not laid the cornerstone, of the structure which Betsy was about to rear, I took care they should have the means to settle comfortably, and from his knowledge in horse breeding, John soon prospered there. Very soon after their arrival in the colony and precisely at the expiration of the usual period from my first entrance within her, she presented her husband with a son. She never had another child.

FINIS